THE DIFFERENCE

We're all different. When Ismae was born, her difference was just easier to see . . .
On a January morning, Beth and Steve bring three-day-old Ismae home from the hospital. Their second child: a little girl to complete their suburban family. Except Ismae is different. She has Down syndrome. As Mae grows up alongside her adoring older brother Al, Beth and Steve must contend with the local Mummy Mafia and tactless relatives — all the while learning to know their daughter. Then a terrible discovery is made. As her marriage begins to crumble, Beth knows she must make an important decision . . .

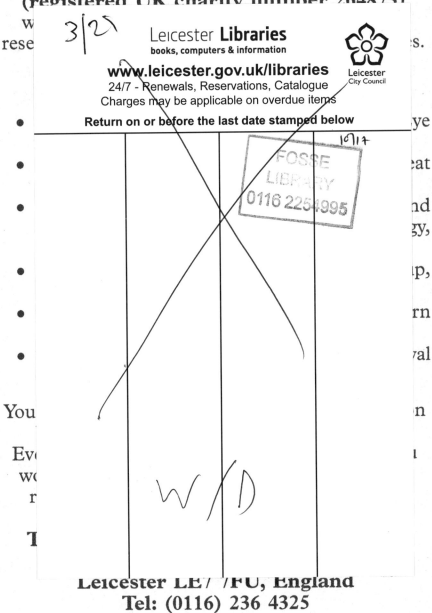

Justine Delaney Wilson read English at Trinity College Dublin and completed a post-grad in Journalism at the Dublin Institute of Technology. She has been writing on a freelance basis ever since, and has worked in television research and production for over a decade.

Twitter — @justinedelw

JUSTINE DELANEY WILSON

◆

THE
DIFFERENCE

Complete and Unabridged

ULVERSCROFT
Leicester

First published in Great Britain in 2016 by
Hachette Books Ireland
Dublin

First Large Print Edition
published 2017
by arrangement with
Hachette Books Ireland
A division of Hachette UK Ltd
Dublin

A catalogue record for this book is available
from the British Library.

ISBN 978–1–4448–3411–6

Published by
F. A. Thorpe (Publishing)
Anstey, Leicestershire

Set by Words & Graphics Ltd.
Anstey, Leicestershire
Printed and bound in Great Britain by
T. J. International Ltd., Padstow, Cornwall

This book is printed on acid-free paper

To my mother Deborah,
for all that you do.

I have noticed that doing the sensible thing is only a good idea when the decision is quite small. For the life-changing things, you must risk it.

Jeanette Winterson
author of Why Be Happy When
You Could Be Normal?

1986

'I'm going to give you an internal first so I need you to pull your knees up and drop them open.'

I tried to relax my clenched legs.

'Will it hurt?'

The nurse's hands were cold and rough.

'Probably about as much as having sex for the first time.'

I tried to think of a grown-up reply but my eyes filled with tears, making me feel even younger than I was.

Through the gaps around the old sash window, I heard the prayers start up again outside. Another girl arriving. The nurse pushed my legs down and pulled up my jumper.

'A bit cold, Beth.' Matter-of-fact, as she squirted gel on my stomach.

'That's OK. I don't mind.' I didn't want to be any trouble.

'There she is. Nine weeks, three days.' I could hear the scan being printed. 'I'm just going to staple this to your file. It makes it easier for the doctor if he can see where everything is before he starts.'

* ★ ★ ★

I was in an old house with a heavy door that had been painted a deep blue. I recognised the blue from the ad at the back of my magazine. It was just one house in the middle of a street of similar houses in Ealing but I knew it was the place as soon as we turned the corner. I could see people with placards on the pavement outside. Enormous, fuzzy scans of foetuses — speech bubbles crudely drawn on them with black marker: 'Why don't you want me, Mummy?'

A small group gathered around the door of our taxi when we pulled up, thrusting pamphlets at me before I could get my feet onto the ground. The picture on the front had been digitally altered to show a dark blobby mass with the formed face and engaging eyes of a robust older baby — 'I love you, Mummy' was written across the bottom. My boyfriend James took it from my trembling hands and threw it behind him into the car before shutting the door on it. A man in a grey polo-neck said nothing but held his toddler up for me to look at.

Head down, I made my way up the path. James carried my bag, his left hand on my shoulder steering me in front of him through the parting crowd. I could feel their eyes on me, wicked with scorn.

I would've run but I knew I'd just be sent back again.

A middle-aged woman jumped in ahead of me and, facing the door, stood square in front of it to block my path. She was thick-set and crammed into a pair of mottled grey tracksuit pants and a tight black T-shirt that made a stack of tyres of her back. Behind me, people started to pray aloud.

Hail Mary, full of grace

The Lord is with Thee

We were two seventeen-year-olds who had come to London to damn our souls.

Blessed art Thou amongst women

'Excuse me, please.' James was hesitant, tapping the lady politely on her round shoulder as though she didn't realise we wanted to get by.

And blessed is the fruit

There was the sound of a bolt sliding across and then the black, strong arms of a security man were reaching out, forcing her to move to one side. His hands found mine and pulled me in through the blue door, which I saw now was badly chipped and peeling.

★ ★ ★

5

In a sitting room that served as the reception area, ordinary girls like me sat and smiled nervously at each other, waiting to be called upstairs, trying not to change their minds. Even the two who were quietly sobbing lifted their curious heads and half-smiled each time the door was opened. Some were alone, some with women I took to be their mothers. James was the only boy.

The next batch of six girls was called. Mine was the third name out. I'd forgotten to give a false one like I'd been told.

⋆   ⋆   ⋆

Dressed in paper robes and discreetly holding maternity pads and pants, each of us sat on big grey leather single-seaters that tilted back like dentists' chairs. A Filipino nurse bustled quietly at a table in the middle. The window was shut and there was nothing to see but the tops of the trees against the grey sky. Nobody spoke. The television was on but the sound had been turned down. At the end of the room was a glass-panelled door that led to a tiny porch area, and through there I could make out swing doors to somewhere that didn't bear thinking about.

The girl two to my right, nearest the porch, was sent for first. I turned and watched her go through the first door, marvelling that her legs could take her there. After a few minutes, I heard older voices — introducing, chatting. Then movement and the voices fading. Silence.

The girl next to me was called soon after. She padded down to the porch in her stockinged feet. Almost immediately, I heard a knock. I saw her tight fist rapping on a swing door — soft and slow at first, then louder and more urgent. The door opened and there was another voice: questioning, warning. I could make out the girl's noisy tears and apologies. She came back into the room rubbing her hand across her flushed face, took up her bag and clothes and whispered to the nurse. The four of us stared at her from our leather recliners. Then she was gone. My hero.

'Beth O'Connor.'

I walked unsteadily to the panelled door and pushed through it.

Just don't think about it.

I saw now that there was a small pew in the porch area. I felt scared and needed to stand up, to move about, but I sat down on it — my pants and pad in my hand — because I thought this was what I was supposed to do.

Tomorrow everything will be back the way it was.

The doors swung open. They were theatre doors, I saw now.

'Beth, hello there. Come on in. How're you feeling?'

A nurse with a Scottish accent smiled broadly as she patted the bed. I felt the draught move my hair as the doors shut behind me. I sat up on the bed and leaned over onto my side to avoid seeing anything. I was shaking and felt cold.

'It'll all be over soon,' she said.

I nodded.

James isn't ready to be a father.

She put her hand on mine and gave it a quick squeeze.

It's for the best. I'm just too young.

'Hello. Another girl from Ireland, I see.' An older man came toward me carrying my file. He was dressed in scrubs, his mask down around his neck revealing a soft face that reminded me of my father's.

I wondered if he had children and what he told them he did for a living.

'You're my second Irish girl already this morning.'

★ ★ ★

When I came around, I was back in the room with the recliners and the silent television.

The three girls to my left were sleeping now, wrapped in blue fleece blankets, their faces relaxed. I saw that my chest and legs had been carefully swaddled too. The chair to my right was still empty. The girl who had been first to go through the doors was dressed and sitting up having tea and biscuits.

Seeing my eyes open, the Filipino nurse came toward me. She handed me the Christmas edition of an interiors magazine from the previous year.

'Thank you.' I laid it on my lap and tried to ignore the cramp gnawing at my insides and what it meant.

A young doctor came in and the dressed girl stood up and went to him. Their conversation was whispered as he gave her a pamphlet with *Aftercare* written on it in large, curly red letters. She extended her hand and he shook it briskly. When their hands parted, she turned to get her things so she didn't see how he wiped his right palm on the front of his trousers before leaving the room.

The girl raised her arms high above her head to wriggle into her tight leather jacket, revealing the tanned, narrow waist that was hers to keep.

★   ★   ★

'Hi, Beth.'

James stood up as he saw me coming down the stairs. He was in reception, his skinny frame obscured by the huge bunch of flowers in his arms.

'I got these for you. But I don't know what I was thinking. Are they OK? I mean, I don't want you to think I'm celebrating, that we're celebrating.'

'They're grand. Thanks.'

'They probably won't let you take them onto the plane though.'

'No. Probably not, but thanks.' My voice was groggy and broken.

I handed him my bag and took the flowers and smelled them. They had no scent.

'Might look a bit mad arriving home from a trip to London with flowers,' I heard myself say.

He smiled uncertainly and the braces on his teeth glistened in the light.

★　★　★

I had a quick read of my aftercare pamphlet in a cubicle in the airport toilets. I skipped straight to the part about the risk of clots and haemorrhaging and did my best to memorise the warning signs.

I dumped it and the flowers into the bin in

the toilets and quickly bought a beefeater magnet and some English shortbread from the stand in Duty Free.

There was a girl I recognised from the clinic on the plane.

I wondered if she was bleeding as heavily as I was.

★   ★   ★

Another taxi, another front door. As we pulled into the driveway, I saw my mother's silhouette come to block my path this time, patting her hair, waiting in the darkness of the front step.

'There you are. Let me see you.' She tilted my face toward the light from the hall. 'You've enough make-up on; that's good. I was worried you'd look a bit pale and your father would notice.'

She spoke quietly, her hands staying on my cheeks. I thought her eyes looked kind. She kissed my forehead.

'It's for the best. You are just too young. We all are,' she whispered into my ear.

My eyes filled as she pulled away and half-turned backwards.

'Dad! Beth's home! From her day in London!' she yelled, her voice shrill and taut.

She motioned James and me into the hall,

commandeering my bag, taking the souvenir magnet and shortbread from my hands, moving life along.

'Come and tell us all about it, darlings. Did you see Buckingham Palace? What *did* you get up to?'

★   ★   ★

My mother and I never spoke about it again. From time to time, little flashes of what I'd done disturbed my thoughts and I'd wonder if the piper would ever want paying.

Twenty-four years later, I'd almost managed to forget.

And then my daughter was born.

My God, the suburbs! They encircled the city's boundaries like enemy territory and we thought of them as a loss of privacy, a cesspool of conformity and a life of indescribable dreariness . . .

John Cheever

Star-Shaped Stars

I live in my hometown again, which is a fact of almost constant disappointment to me.

It was my choice, one I think I was excited about when I made it almost four years ago and thought that what was familiar was desirable. It's only minutes from my parents' home so there are some of the conveniences I'd imagined, but mostly it's a glaring indication of how far I haven't got.

I look out our bedroom window here in Vesey Hill and see how quickly the view stops, the vista so narrow and slight even though this suburb is raised above the town. From here it's impossible to have any sense of what might be going on in the city, or even a mile away. Nothing but big houses, like ours, keeping the world at bay with their chests pushed out and their shoulders broad with importance. In the distance, I can just make out the tops of the grand gates which mark the boundary of the estate.

From the outside, the houses of Vesey Hill are identical. I'd wager there isn't a riot of difference between them inside either for that matter, but I can't be sure. From our front door, the two opposite look back at us. Unresponsive. In each of them, three straight-edged cream-coloured blinds in the windows upstairs sit exactly midway up, giving them the appearance of half-closed eyelids.

My husband, Steve, is from New Zealand so moving there was always a possibility. When we first met, he often spoke of the future. I'd move nearer him, be attentive with every cell of my being, as though physically leaning toward the conversation would make me part of its potential. His dreams involved a sail boat, a house by the sea, and work he enjoyed, back there.

And me, if I would like that.

We built this dream life together in our heads, colouring in every tiny detail.

That was fourteen years ago.

He paved a section in the back garden to house a giant barbecue and a few easy chairs last month, to recreate 'a little bit of the Kiwi lifestyle'. The damp Irish summer has prevented us from using the barbecue for anything other than standing our eleven-year-old son Al's Wellington boots on until the mud hardens and can be chipped off. Wearing a jacket out on his paving, my husband is hopeful about the possibility of a more rousing future for the three of us where he calls home.

I say that I'm easy, like the chairs.

If we did live in New Zealand, with its clean, wide streets, I'd get to be the exotic one. I could reinvent myself any way I pleased. In my fantasies, I'd have a rewarding life because I'd deserve it after sacrificing my homeland for my husband. And as the foreigner, I couldn't be blamed if things didn't work out.

Steve has been the foreign one for so long. His accent causes heads to tilt and smiles to be raised. Once on a flight from Dublin to Rome, he asked the older lady next to him if he could borrow a pen. She lifted her powdered face and smiled.

'You're not from here now, are you?' and immediately reached to oblige this man with the dark colouring and the antipodean lilt. His accent thickened as he smiled back and answered her.

She rooted through a huge leather travel bag. 'I'm quite certain I have one in here.' No pocket went unzipped, no snappy glasses case unopened. She marvelled at his every utterance while persisting with the awkward digging. After an age of struggled burrowing, she sat upright, pushed her tinsel-silver hair back from her face, and gave out a triumphant, 'I *knew* I had one.' In her right hand, held aloft, was a safety pin.

Sometimes when I think about the possibility of moving there, I feel exhilarated. As though I might actually say a big 'I do' to life's proposal. As though there are a million possible ways my life might go. Even two.

We'd moved to London after Al was born, full of love and enthusiasm. Just for a couple of years, we'd said. We had our beautiful plans for a sail boat and the sea and a life on the other side of the world. A seven-year lucky streak on Steve's boom-time salary later, his job offered change again and an opportunity to move back to Dublin.

Not part of the sail-boat plans but a chance for me to move my life back to Ireland, to settle our son into school and among family. My mother was sure we needed to do this for Al. That my job as a copywriter — 'What does that even *mean*, Beth? It doesn't sound like any career I've ever heard of' — precluded me from being a good mother and a supportive wife to my important husband. It just wasn't possible to do it all long-term, she said, which is why she had never done it at all. That Al was losing out on being raised in a noisy city, without family around him, and his father travelling with his successful career and his mother out *working* too, she said. The poor child! I should mark her words.

We came back to Ireland and, not long

after, it felt like there'd been a death. Not of a very close loved one but the loss of something vital all the same. Something that couldn't be caught hold of. We'd everything we needed in this big house and we were near the things that I'd been told were necessary in order to cope, to live a grown-up life, to allow me be an attentive mother, so Steve could still travel and be important and satisfied, so Al could flourish.

But routine and housing estates and school gates and being a daughter again scoured our gloss away and the sail-boat dream faded like an old photograph left in a damp and forgotten place.

Time has skittered past by four years and everything feels insubstantial. Except for this house, which seems to be gaining on us. Locking us in.

My courage has shrivelled alongside my cul-de-sac existence. And now, most of the time, the other side of the world just seems a very long way away.

But I will say this: of all the countries I've travelled to in my life, I've never seen stars like those that shine over New Zealand. Actual star-shaped stars, powerful and spellbinding and eager to be wished on in an inky dark sky.

Sitting Still

Not for the first time, I was sitting with my head shrink-wrapped in Tesco cling film thinking that there were few things more depressingly suburban than having your hair done in a neighbour's kitchen. Regular household items are innovatively employed by the stylist while ladies nod their dripping heads and make impressed noises; just tear your regular tin foil into strips to make — *tah dah!* — foil strips, just like in a proper salon, only jagged and uneven and a bit short.

'Is that water too hot for you?'

Cupping her hands to fill them under the tap and dumping the lukewarm contents on my head, with every few splashes I could feel one of Audrey's nails catch the side of my face.

'No, no, it's grand. Thanks.'

The row of bangles on her left wrist clanged against each other every second. I had a pain in my neck already from bending it over the porcelain sink.

'Your layers have grown real long since I saw you last, haven't they? I'll take a good bit off them.'

A toddler pulled on my sleeve before I got a chance to answer.

'Mummy, how long more?'

'Your mummy's over there, darling, in front of the telly,' I answered without looking. Moirah would be waiting for her colour to take for another while so I knew where she'd be stationed.

A pause while she looked over.

'That's not my mummy.'

I hinged my neck up, causing water to run down my back. 'It is, honey. She just has special cream and foil on her head so she looks a bit funny. See, she's wearing her white trousers. And she looks like you, with her big brown eyes.'

★ ★ ★

I sat on a stool at the kitchen island to wait to have my errant layers dealt with, while Audrey went to check on Moirah.

'I don't know myself since I got it wired with electricity.' Rachel's voice came from behind me.

It took me a moment to realise she was referring to the island.

'Oh, yes,' I said. 'I imagine it's very handy.'

'Oh, you've no idea. It's changed my life. You should get yours wired. Saoirse and Kate both had it done recently and when I saw theirs, I just had to have it. Kate's island *is* a bit smaller though because she still has the original kitchen.'

She had lowered her voice and mouthed the last two words, imparting a message that she expected I'd understand.

'I think we might have the original kitchen too,' I said back.

'No, no! No, you don't. Caroline and Andrew who lived there before you were *very good* about updating. She had new cupboards and a bigger island fitted a couple of years back, when most of us did.'

'I'll mention it to Steve,' I said, to end the conversation.

I could see Anna and Saoirse in the adjacent sunroom with their slick heads waiting to be blow dried. Anna was talking Saoirse through her eight-year-old son Luke's birthday party the previous weekend, sliding along the photos on her phone, one frame at a time. Anna pointed her arms skyward to demonstrate just how high the 'unbelievable' pyramid display of cupcakes was; a synchronised swimmer with her wet hair, bare, straight arms and pinched face.

'It cost an absolute fortune, but he loved it. He was delighted with himself. And the other mums were all taking pictures so it was definitely worth it.'

'You can't put a price on their happiness, can you?'

'No, you can't. And everyone was commenting on it.'

'Oh,' said Saoirse, as Anna slid the next picture across the screen. 'Is that the lady from next door? See — at the back there? The new one. Did you invite her?'

'Who? Sommer? No, no. I don't know her at all and, to be honest with you, I didn't think Muslims went to parties. She just came in with her younger boy — I think his name is Ibrahim, or something — to give Luke a present. They didn't stay.'

'I think Muslims do go to parties, they just don't drink.'

'I'm just not sure what we'd all have in common with her. She seems perfectly fine but she always seems to be smiling. I suppose that could be the innocence of an oppressive religion. Don't get me wrong, I've no problem with their beliefs or anything,' she said airily.

'Apparently he's a doctor, you know. Her husband. Janine Woods at the school told me that.'

'I had heard that, yes. But even so, Robert and I don't like to encourage renters.'

A couple of hours had passed since we'd arrived into the corner house at the pylon end of the street and now four out of five ladies were finished and waiting. Audrey liked to do five heads on a morning — 'any more and I can't give you all the individual attention you deserve'. The four of us with the completed heads held onto our empty teacups with one hand while we pressed the last of our scone crumbs with the middle fingers of the other and made a meal out of them. Leaving before all heads are coiffed is frowned upon and word of your bad breeding will spread to the extent that you might lose your seat in the taxi booking for the Christmas night out.

Out of the silence, Rachel started reading aloud from the Residents' Association letter that had come through our letterboxes the previous evening. It threatened to 'name and shame' any dog seen fouling the neighbourhood. She was suddenly incensed: 'Quite right too. They should take those fucking dogs' photos.'

Sitting at her electrical island, half-listening to her rant, I tried to age Rachel. She couldn't have been more than thirty-five, maybe four or five years younger than me. Had she always been like this? How had I come to be part of this world of linen trousers and mean chat?

It seemed like no length ago that I was lying on the floor in the lounge of my city-centre flat with the TV turned up to block out the sounds of my flatmate Jilly in the bathroom. She and I lived together for over three years in what was essentially one large room that had been sectioned by cheap plywood into four barely human-sized boxes — kitchen/lounge, bathroom, two bedrooms. The four boxes were divided, cross-like, by the world's narrowest corridor. If I raised my elbows they would touch off the walls on each side. Sprung doors barely opened into beds and naked lightbulbs swung when they banged shut. The whole place gave health and safety the two fingers.

If Jilly brought someone home with her, I'd be woken during the night by the sound of him bumping down the corridor and I'd have to listen to him peeing. It seemed a peculiarly intimate thing to overhear so keenly, given that I'd yet to see his face. But the plywood didn't allow for any secrets.

Back then, I considered public transport around the city to be among the greatest of life's cruelties. Leaking earphones, wet umbrellas, and overfilled backpacks crowding in, filling every silence and space. Some late nights, Jilly and I would walk home across town and we'd giggle at the stupor of faces passing us in the glowering windows of the night bus.

I'd have given anything for a little bit of room and my own transport.

Now I had a five-bedroomed detached house and was part of a three-person, two-car family. But I was without any real sense of possibility.

I haven't seen Jilly in over a decade. All I know about her is that she lives in north Wicklow with a man called Colm. I know this because a couple of Christmases ago I received the first of several cards from her with two names inside — 'Love Jilly and Colm' — both written in her handwriting. On the flap of the envelope was a shiny gold sticker that gave their postal address in italicised black lettering. We've never met Colm but, having seen the envelopes, it's clear to my mother that Jilly has 'done very well for herself'.

My thoughts were disturbed by the sound of the can of hairspray being put down with a flourish that said the ceremony was over. We all stood.

'That's it, girls. All done for another month or so. You look gorgeous.'

'Will you have a cup of tea before you go,

Audrey?' asked Rachel.

Please God, don't boil that kettle again.

'Ah no. I'll let you all get back to it.'

The four of us who didn't live there made noises about this and that, just to fill the air while we pretended not to be organising our money. Hands made opening, closing and folding motions in the darkened space inside expensive bags. I saw Anna's eyes narrow trying to make out what others were giving. She had her notes ready: a tiny, hard square made at home this morning before she came.

'Thanks so much. Thanks. Ah, you're very good.'

'Did you enjoy it? It was a nice morning, wasn't it?' Rachel was asking me, looking straight into my eyes.

'Yes, lovely. Definitely. And great value.'

'Isn't it? I always say that to Garry. It's great value. And so convenient.'

Anna answered, 'Absolutely. I didn't even have to turn the oven off while I ran across. You look fab.'

Then Saoirse, 'Peter won't know me when he gets home. We'll have to go out. Can't waste it!'

'Oh no, you can't waste it now. You look gorgeous.' Audrey admired her own work.

Then my voice, 'That style really suits you.'

'Thanks. Yours does too, Beth,' was returned.

27

We were neighbours, not friends, so the compliments were standard and meaningless.

★ ★ ★

I walked across the street to my green front door feeling ridiculously free. I shut it behind me, made a stab at fixing my hair in the hall mirror and swore Never Again.

Usually I forget and, one morning a month or so later, the phone rings to remind me. They can see my car in the driveway. And I'm not known for my walks. If the friendliest neighbour wanted to put her face right up to my side window and block the sun with her hands, she'd be able to make out my silhouette sitting on the stairs.

The Pleasure Was All Yours

We pulled into my parents' drive where we were met by my mother struggling to get her arms into her blazer.

Al, Steve and I stood with her in the driveway while my father locked up the house. We were going to the Mothering Sunday Luncheon at the golf club. It was my mother's idea and there was little room for manoeuvre given the day that was in it. We were all to travel in our car together, also her idea. 'It'll be such *fun*,' she had said.

The only other mother of the group, I didn't particularly want to spend Sunday afternoon at Woodford. I knew it wasn't Al's idea of a good time either but so far he hadn't said anything. He'd made a beautiful card and given it to me that morning with my breakfast in bed. 'I know you'll be wiping specks of glitter off stuff for the next week, which is kind of annoying for you, but it didn't look as good without it,' he'd said.

He was eleven years old now and overthought most things.

He handed my mother the small bunch of white tulips I had bought for her earlier.

'Thank you, Alex, my darling. How gorgeous.' She laid them down on the step outside the locked front door. 'I shall arrange them as soon as we get back. Now then — in we get.' The last part was meant to sound like a cheery suggestion but I could hear the order not quite managing to hide. Bending herself almost in half, she got into the back of the car head first. She clambered across three spaces and took up her position at the far door.

'It'll be fogacious,' Al said to nobody in particular as he followed her in to the middle space. This was a word of his own and had its root in the noun 'fogey'. Since its creation last week, he'd already had cause to use it several times around his grandmother.

'Not at all. Don't be silly, Alex.' Keeping her voice jolly and reapplying her lipstick in a compact mirror.

I sat into the back of the car beside Al. My father was in the front passenger seat punching the buttons that would have changed the radio station had the key been in the ignition yet. Steve got into the driver's seat.

The five of us in, we fastened our belts and drove toward carvery boredom.

★   ★   ★

Woodford wasn't a relaxed place, which largely suited the members. It was charmlessly self-conscious with its crazy amount of silver cutlery and mind-your-manners pretensions. And yet you didn't have to look far for canteen-type slips: the lurid-coloured sauce sachets stuffed into stainless steel sugar bowls as centrepieces; the lighting, which would have perfectly illuminated an area for security purposes.

I knew it was going to be a long afternoon as soon as we stepped inside. The club was packed. Plates were being held aloft by older ladies ambling around dressed for a shift in a casino: burgundy-coloured waistcoats, black dickie bows, white shirts and short black skirts, which were tight across the stomach.

We stood in the middle of the floor waiting for one of these croupiers to notice us and direct us to our table. They noticed us all right but sauntered on by, narrowly avoiding well-dressed children chasing each other with forks. Plates of salmon fillet drowned in vivid yellow viscous fluid or huge slices of greying meat dying in pale gravy passed from time to time.

The service was always desperately slow at Woodford, not that you could say it. My parents were devout members and took any criticism of it as a personal insult.

31

'There's a lovely, warm ambience,' I heard my mother say, perhaps in response to the screams of a child — who had been hunkered up on her seat to better yell at someone under the table — losing her balance and falling to the ground as her chair tipped backwards. I almost said that the room might have benefited from some background music.

'How about I get us all drinks!' Steve said, mustering enthusiasm, and quickly took himself off to the bar area.

'I'll go with Dad.' Al scurried after him.

To get to our seats, we had to step over a baby dressed in a cream babygro who lay supine on the floor between our table and that of her round-faced family. 'Blow-ins with no manners,' my father proclaimed. The baby — a girl, I guessed, by her soft eyes and little bow mouth — was awake but her chubby face was all that moved, so intrigued or stupefied was she by the goings-on around her. I met her eyes and she surprised me by holding my gaze with an unimpressed expression. '*What are we doing here?*' her face asked. '*No idea,*' I found myself shrugging back as I sat down.

A glamorous-looking woman in her mid-fifties approached us, her eyes wide to convey some kind of delight. She introduced herself to my father the way someone does when they think the person must *surely* know them and is merely *pretending* to need reminding. She was wearing the kind of dress that a woman could easily make friends in, if it were male friends of a certain vintage she was after. It plunged ill-advisedly down between her aging breasts and made it impossible not to stare at her turkey décolleté.

'Dolores Norton,' she said loudly to the rest of us and thrust her hand out for someone to take. I reached for it, in case nobody else did. My father was confused and did little to hide it.

She put her hands on her hips, mock-scolding him, and motioned at the table nearest the door where a group of octogenarians were noisily debating the menu with squinted eyes and creaking voices.

'I'm Bill's daughter — his youngest daughter, Dolores.' She was addressing my father directly, her hand resting on his arm, just above his wrist.

'Of course. Yes, Dolores,' he answered.

My mother said nothing but looked away, unfolding and folding the napkin on her lap.

Dolores started into a loud and lengthy monologue about her recent travels to India, which was 'not as dirty as one might expect'. She brought a strange vibrancy to this dog-eared room but was already very annoying company. Not that she'd have cared what I thought. It was clear that my father's attention was all she wanted from our table.

Dolores was talking about 'dear friends' of hers who lived 'all over the world' when I noticed my mother turning one of her earrings in its hole every minute and straightening her jacket by tugging its lapels. She only had two real friends and they both lived within three miles of her house.

Dolores had finished speaking and was lingering, waiting for someone to introduce a new topic. My mother poured herself some more wine. Al and Steve started playing Xs and Os on a napkin. I looked over at the carpet larva, who looked back at me.

'Well, lovely to talk to you, Dermot,' she said after a moment.

'The pleasure was all yours,' my father said, smiling. She laughed animatedly and play-slapped him on the shoulder — '*Oh, you*' — not realising that he meant it.

Our food arrived and was of the calibre that you might expect to get in a staff cafeteria if you worked in a supermarket. I saw that each option came with three scooped hills of mashed potatoes and a cereal bowl full of sweetcorn and bevelled carrot coins.

I thought of a dinner with Eoin, an old boyfriend of mine, in a very formal restaurant when I was about twenty-three. When we were seated, I looked down at cutlery stretching all the way from my anxious hands to the edge of the table, on both sides. I saw that he was surveying his too. And then he pushed all of these silver soldiers into a pile with his right hand. With one swift movement, knives, forks, and spoons of various heights and widths were humbled. Just eating utensils, without mystery or rank. When the various courses arrived, he picked and chose from this pile as he pleased. Its still one of the sexiest things I've ever seen. A lifetime ago.

I looked up and saw that Steve was looking at me.

My father was wrapping up a story when my mind returned to the table. 'I knew it. I knew that once the wooden house went up in flames, that family wouldn't have a chance. They'd all perish, no question. And what happened? Not one of them got out in time.'

There was nothing he liked more than being proven right, regardless of how unfortunate the circumstances.

'Those tiny windows upstairs and all that wood. I said it. I bloody said it. A whole family wiped out. But sure, some people can't be told.'

He pushed away his plate to signal he was finished eating and took out his new phone.

'Do you see this, Alex? I'm the first person around here to have one of these phones.'

I didn't know whether he meant in the club or the postal district. He jabbed at the screen a few times and frowned.

'EUGENE!' he roared across the room.

'Grandad, aren't phones banned in here? Unless you're a doctor or something?'

'He can't hear me — EUGENE!'

A man I took to be Eugene gave him a small wave of sorts from behind the bar and went back to drying glasses.

'What's the Wi-Fi code in here? He still can't hear me.'

'I think everyone else can,' Steve said.

'THE WI-FI CODE. EUGENE! WHAT IS IT?'

Most of the room turned to look at Eugene.

Al passed me a napkin. On it he had written, 'Mortified'.

I smiled, but my smile had a subtext: *I know. Just sit it out.* He read it correctly and slumped back in his chair to suck on his gums.

*   *   *

On the way home in the car, my mother was telling us how we'd all had a wonderful time

36

— a lovely afternoon'.

When we got out at my parents' house I saw the tulips had been rained on but were bearing up. My mother lifted them and set about trying to dry them with her sleeve. She and Al went into the kitchen where he held them while she found a vase. I watched her fill it with too much water, definitely enough to make them blow out, droop and die prematurely. But I didn't say anything. She would know best.

The Scar

'Tell me a story, something that I don't already know about you,' Steve had said.

We were fifteen minutes into our first date together.

'You don't know anything about me.' I bought time, trying to think of something more interesting than the others before me would have said.

He was dressed like a slacker, in low-rise jeans and layered skinny tops, and he looked gorgeous for it in the way twenty-something men can. He spoke clearly, but softly. I'd noticed his habit of adding a question mark to the end of his sentences. His voice inflected, looking for encouragement to go on, coaxing me to stay with him while he spoke. It was endearing, as every new discovery is, at the start.

Having looked at the menu, we both decided on the crabmeat salad and said so together. I was of the youthful frame of mind that saw this as serendipity, a signal of something that was Meant to Be.

'Where did you get the scar on your chin?' He threw me a bone.

I stretched back my head and with the fingers of my right hand traced the route of the sixteen-year-old scar that ran down my chin toward the base of my neck. So much for it not being that visible anymore.

'In France,' I said, as though I had chosen it whilst experiencing Europe as a student. 'Many years ago,' I started, 'my parents and I spent eighteen queasy hours on a ferry before driving half the length of France in my dad's new green MGB car.'

I remembered the car's fold-back roof and how, when I tilted my head back onto the head rest, I'd had to close my eyes against the glare of the rushing sun, a perfect round ball leading the car. My thighs in shorts were stuck to the warm blue leatherette of the back seat. My father drove while my mother sat next to him stroking her belly, seven months pregnant. My father patted her hand when he stopped at the traffic lights.

'Perhaps it wasn't that hot — I was only eight' — Steve's nod and shrug agreed — 'but I remember rolling my empty glass Orangina bottle across my forehead until it seemed to be sweating like I was. When the car stopped, I peeled myself off the seat and made for the playground I'd seen as we entered the site. Behind me, my parents admired the tent-house-thing that we'd parked outside.

Oh, Dermot, look! Plastic windows with curtains!

Camping has come a long way, Johanna. I told you. Sure, you could live in this.

'I ran straight for the swings, wanting to whip up some air, to feel something cool on my legs. And I remember the sensation of flight as I sailed up off the little wooden seat and then down toward the ground. I landed flat on the tarmac, my chin and neck taking the weight of my head, my sun-burnt shoulders up around my ears. I lay like a caterpillar, you know — body out behind me.'

Steve stopped chewing and put his bread roll down.

'I could hear noise, a screaming into the distance. I knew it wasn't coming from me — my whole body was leaning on my jaw. I hadn't thought that anybody knew I was there, but the site was busy so I suppose people must've seen. I'm not sure what happened then but we were back in the car, the campsite manager with us this time, Dad being directed to a small doctor's surgery some distance away.'

'Small doctor or small surgery?' Steve smiled.

'Small surgery. Tall doctor, as it turned out.'

I remembered my mother holding me in

the back, reassuring and soothing. My father was driving nervously, asking if I'd be OK, worrying aloud. But she calmed the situation, telling me gentle jokes and singing Elvis's 'Good Luck Charm' quietly. She was different back then. Capable.

'When we arrived at the surgery, which was indeed very small, my father opened his car door and promptly passed out onto the ground outside.' Steve hooted at this and resumed chewing. 'Which is where he was left while the campsite manager carried me in, my waddling mother behind us, looking back at her husband who had succumbed to sunstroke and stress.

'Inside, the doctor set about stitching my chin and asked my mother to hold the tray of implements. *Whereupon*,' I paused and Steve widened his eyes, 'she fainted too — slumped straight to the ground.'

I could see her, in my mind's eye, lying on the marble floor like a pregnant rag doll in a lemon sundress.

'I was left with thread dangling from my face, while she was lifted onto a bed.'

'Jeez. What a family.' He picked up his bread roll again.

'All three of us were hospitalised, probably just to keep us out of harm's way. We hadn't been five minutes at the site.'

Steve and I were laughing together, potential stretching out ahead of us like an open road.

We had met in a nightclub the previous weekend. I'd noticed him because he was looking directly at me. I planted myself at the side of the dance floor, as though in a queue for something, and waited for him to act on his stare.

He had asked me to go home with him later that night: 'I'll light the fire for you.'

'No.'

'It's a real fire, you know. And it's no small thing lighting it. But I'm prepared to do it for you.'

'No.' But I was smiling then.

'You're quite right. Absolutely. I admire that,' he had said.

'But I will. Maybe next time,' I'd felt the need to add.

I wondered if he was thinking about this when our knees touched under the table and he smirked into his crab salad.

So I didn't finish my story.

I didn't tell him that soon after I got the scar on my chin, my mother's baby — my brother — was stillborn.

Lines and Tigers

'I think your car might need to be serviced. It seems a bit noisy.'

My mother and I were in the Ford Puma my father had bought her eight years ago. She had quite liked the look of herself in it then. The atrocious racket from it now meant that she wore a tense scowl while driving it. On the upside it awarded us the brief freedom to shout at each other.

'Well, it's not going to be as quiet as your father's and you're more used to going places with him. He likes to take care of that car.'

'We'll have to drop it into the garage this week. You can't be going around in this.'

'Things can get bloody noisy when they're neglected,' she roared.

★ ★ ★

It was just after 7 p.m. on a Tuesday evening. A picture of my mother smiling — her highlighted hair held back by a Burberry sun visor — had flashed on the screen of my mobile phone just minutes before.

Putting her on loudspeaker and turning the

volume up full, I'd managed to make out her words between sobs.

'It's Sarah. I spoke to her daughter Gemma. I don't think she has long left. I'd like to go to see her before visiting hours close at eight and I can't get hold of your father.'

'Oh, Mum. I'm sorry to hear that. Are you at home?'

'Of course I am.' Bitter, even in sorrow.

'We'll go as soon as I get there.'

She was already in her car with the engine running when I arrived at the house. I sat into the passenger seat and saw that she was wearing her belted-up tweed coat and that she had her going-out jewellery on.

*   *   *

We walked down the corridor of St Ita's wing, my mother a few paces ahead of me, head up, body full of purpose. She followed large plastic arrows directing visitors toward the various saints. The click-clacking of our shoes seemed loud, rude even, as we moved away from the wards and nearer to her best friend. She was in the hushed part of the hospital, where people lay in dimly lit single rooms without flowers or grapes, their families telling them kind lies about when

44

they'd be back at home in their own beds.

When we saw Room 3 a little up ahead on the right, she stopped and I caught up with her.

A man appeared from the left and stretched out his hand to shake my mother's. When he took mine, I saw he had the drained look of a concerned relative. He steered us both in through a door on the left that had a blue 1 over it.

'He's comfortable and less agitated today. They've upped his medication.'

Then more loudly, and with breaks between the words, 'Dad, look. You have two visitors. Look who has come to see you.'

My mother gave a little benign nod in the direction of the bed and then turned a crazed expression on me.

He thinks we're here to see his father — her eyes screamed.

Yes, I got that — mine replied.

An old and fragile face, its skull barely heavy enough to make an indent in the over-stuffed hospital pillow, turned very slightly to look at us.

'He doesn't look himself without his teeth in. He looks a bit sunken today.' The son pressed his own cheeks in with his thumb and third finger to demonstrate. 'But it's just without the teeth.'

My mother and I made noises of agreement.

His body was covered in blankets, expertly pulled up by a nurse to cover his shoulders and nail down his arms, revealing only sagging flesh hanging either side of a windpipe.

I had never met this man or his son before, and my mother's silence told me she hadn't either. She stood, looking past both men, her eyes fixed on the flashing heartbeat monitor on the side table as though the numbers meant something to her.

The son sat down on one of two plastic orange seats.

I leaned over the old face in the bed.

'It's lovely to see you.' The words, broken and loud, jarred in my ears as I said them.

Two lifeless eyes looked into mine.

A feeling of pity was lead in my stomach. 'I hope they're all looking after you.'

I thought I saw the tiniest of smiles.

'Can I get anything for you?'

I hoped I wasn't speaking too loudly. I wondered if he ever questioned why everyone had started shouting at him once he'd moved into this room.

He held his eyes on mine before moving his face to the left, dragging my gaze across. His eyes came to rest on a string of blue pearl rosary beads that hung on the iron post of the headboard.

'Do you want your beads?'

He closed and opened his eyes. Yes.

'He does. Yes, he does.' My mother behind me nervous and desperate that he should have them.

'Of course. Let me get them.'

I unhooked them with my finger and piled them into my palm. They were cold.

'They are beautiful. Would you like to hold them in your hand?'

Paper-thin eyelids opened and closed again. Definitely a tiny smile.

His son was on his feet, not wasting a moment, heaving the blanket pile back too far, exposing thin, yellowed forearms that disappeared into oversized navy night-shirt sleeves. The man's body was almost flat, his thighs like a hairpin on the white sheet. I saw the right hand open slightly. I wrapped the beads around his hand and closed his fist on them. His eyes shut.

I felt light-headed as I stood back and into my mother, who had moved in close to me. I saw that her eyes were glassy. She squeezed my arm a little and stepped away.

His son fixed the sheet and blankets back up on him, tucking them into the sides of the bed, trying his best to get them the way they had been. They were piled too high at the top under the tiny chin now, obscuring his view.

'Thank you. For that. I never thought about giving him his beads,' he said quietly, sitting back down.

'We should be going.' My head was swaying and I couldn't depend on my legs to support me. I panicked that the comfort of the rosary beads would give the father his cue to leave this life and I didn't want him to die looking up at two strangers. I imagined our awkwardness at his funeral, my mother graciously leaving the explaining to me.

'Oh, yes, OK. Thank you for coming. You're very good.' He stood again.

My mother stepped forward and hugged him briskly. Then she turned and patted the blankets that covered the dying man, his tiny body finished with movement.

I walked on tiptoe out of the room, my mother's shoes clip-clopping behind me.

In the corridor, she stopped in front of the door with the blue 3 above it.

I leaned against the wall on the far side of a steel trolley, worried that the son from the other room might see me.

'I'll wait here for you. Take your time.'

'No, go on down to the café. I wouldn't like that poor young man to see you and realise his mistake. I'll meet you down there.'

'OK, if you're happy you'll find me.' I could feel the cold of the rosary beads on my clammy hands. I rubbed my palms up and down on my jeans a few times and stuck them into my pockets. I needed to sit down.

She nodded brusquely, straightened her shoulders and stepped silently into the room.

★　★　★

My mother outstretched both of her arms as she came toward me in the café, as though it was our habit. I stood up, confused, my arms self-consciously mimicking hers. As we attempted an embrace, I felt her body weight fall and realised she was sobbing. Everyone — the ones in nightgowns and novelty slippers, and the others wearing jackets and jingling car keys — was distracted for a moment by our display.

Quickly, she remembered herself and sat. She took a hanky from her bag, put it over her nose and mouth and closed her eyes. Her voice was quiet and steady when she eventually spoke.

'I wouldn't have known her, Beth. I would have passed her by. Gemma is sitting at the end of the bed rubbing her mother's feet, talking away to her. Brian's doing a crossword, wondering aloud at the clues. But she's oblivious. She's like a tiny shell of herself.'

I looped her hair behind her ear, the way she liked to keep it.

'They were only doing their best to be positive, I suppose. Saying they'd see me in again at the weekend. It'll all be over before then. Anyway. We better get home. Your father will be wondering where I've got to.'

★ ★ ★

'Johanna! Johanna O'Connor! How are you?' A voice came from the doorway of the cloudy circular booth in the lobby where banished smokers sat.

A woman I half-recognised from some-where, probably the golf club, had her foot stuck in the Perspex doorway and was neither in nor out of the booth. Her voice sounded brash and loud, jarring with the hospital setting. Old broken faces looked up from the bench inside.

'Gloria.' I saw my mother jolt a little.

Gloria exhaled back over her shoulder into the booth. 'I'm wonderful, not a bother on me,' she said, answering a question that hadn't been asked. 'Tell me, were you in with Sarah?'

The booth faces turned to my mother. One

moved the wheels of his IV drip to get a better view.

My mother gave a weak smile. 'Yes. Yes, I was.'

'How *does* she look?' Her voice dipped into concern.

'Not too good.'

'The poor lamb. It's just not fair, is it?'

An elderly lady standing behind her in a lavender button-down nightdress shook her head.

Gloria let the door shut in her face and came closer to us, taking a final, urgent drag on her cigarette before putting it out on the floor under her shoe.

'Well, I best get on up there. I want to be home in time for bridge.'

Up close, I saw she was attractive in a careless, confident kind of a way. She wore almost no make-up and her hair fell wild and loose around her shoulders.

'Cheerio, Johanna. I've always loved that coat on you. Oh, and nice to see you too.' She smiled in my direction.

She looked at the butt for a second before she walked away. The look acknowledged that, while she was someone who would leave a cigarette butt on the floor of a hospital, she was decent enough to pretend at some unease about doing it.

★   ★   ★

Back at my parents' house, we sat in the lounge, my mother with her crystal goblet of wine in her hand. I'd resisted hitting the television's On button as I walked by it, much as I'd have welcomed its gaudy intrusion. Glancing at my watch, I noted that the clock on the wall was still ten minutes fast — my mother ever-determined to beat Time.

'She has always admired your father. Sarah, I mean. She used to say that he was the person you would call in a crisis.' My mother swirled the wine dangerously close to the edge of her glass as she spoke.

'You know what I mean, darling: that he's a solid, dependable sort of a man,' she elaborated, inviting me to accept the fact.

I nodded, wondering where he was now.

I looked at the side of her face. She was still a good-looking woman but now, in the lamplight, she looked old, certainly older than she was. At sixty-nine, her face seemed little more than a collection of powdery lines and crevices, as though someone had let the air out of her. I wondered how long her eyes had looked so tired. I imagined it must be draining to always try to be in control, to constantly measure your outbursts, to live with my father.

I thought of his soft face and how relatively unlined it was. He had worked hard at his practice but had been an employer most of his life and always looked after himself. He had the appearance of a man who had the upper hand. It was the people around him who looked haggard.

I knew I should bring up something to talk about, something new to shift her gear. If we were closer, it would have been the perfect opportunity to announce that I thought I was pregnant. But we weren't, and anyway maybe I wasn't.

Although I was pretty sure I was.

'He used to write me little cards, you know. With poems in them.'

She motioned at the black-and-white photo above the clock.

She thought she'd caught me looking at it when I was staring at nothing, thinking of people I knew who had babies at my age.

'Oh, it was a long time ago now.' She dismissed the admission as quickly as she'd made it.

Barbara Whelan from two streets over. She was forty or so. That was it. One. Oh, and that woman from Al's school who'd just had those twins. She looked at least forty, forty-two maybe. But that might just be from lack of sleep. Even the prospect of a baby

53

made me feel tired now. It wasn't what I imagined for my life, for this stage.

But then, very little of how things had gone, of where Steve and I now found ourselves — baby or not — was part of any kind of plan.

I remembered an afternoon only weeks after we had first met, lying on our backs on his bed staring at the ceiling.

'I love you.'

His words so unexpected, so welcome. I said nothing in response and kept my eyes skyward. I wanted to preserve it, that wonderful moment when something small and shiny is becoming something more. Before either of you has made any mistakes.

He turned toward me. 'I do, you know.'

I had moved my face so my eyes could meet his. He was propped up on one elbow peering in at me.

'Say it again then.'

'I love you.'

So long ago.

Back when we shared books, literally — reading at the same pace, me sitting on the right, turning the pages when we finished two. Ridiculously romantic.

We rarely made time to do anything together any more. We had become stale cut-out versions of ourselves. Or at least, I had.

I focused on the photo of my parents. I'd seen it a million times before. They couldn't have been more than twenty-five. They were both grinning, lit from the inside. Back when life was just the two of them.

'I didn't know Dad ever wrote poetry.'

'Oh, yes.' She straightened her back and flicked an imaginary crumb off her chest, recalling her days as a muse. 'He used to hide them for me to find.'

'Do you still have any of them?' I struggled to imagine my father gushing, on paper.

'Oh, they're probably in a box in the attic somewhere. I wouldn't have thrown them out. In a box up there with God knows what.'

Limericks started forming in my head.

I once met a girl called Johanna

'What were they like?'

With yellow hair like a banana.

'They were beautiful.' She looked out the window at her car, which was resting in the driveway having growled at us the whole way home.

She let out an embarrassed little laugh but the voice that followed it was weary.

'Of course, I suppose it's possible that he was hiding them *from* me.'

Clearing Tables

So on a Monday night in January, Ismae Eve O'Connor Rogers came into the world with her eyes open.

To the sound of her fulsome cry, the midwife remarked how rare this was. And how it was believed to be lucky, 'extremely lucky'. Steve and I felt the pride of our daughter's first achievement. I looked out through the rain-splattered dependable windows of the delivery room and thought that having my second child at this stage of my life might not actually be so bad.

★   ★   ★

The following morning, I hid Ismae's face from the kindly woman in the pink apron who wheeled the food cart of boiled eggs around to the beds of the new mothers.

The woman I shared the room with was showing her baby off to staff, nurses, anyone. Pointing out the curtain of dark hair around the back of his head — 'Friar Tuck!' — and telling stories about trying to shave her legs after her waters had broken and her emergency Caesarean. I went out into the hallway and cried. The raw and angry pain of not getting what I'd been expecting, the baby girl I'd imagined, was unbearable. My cries were noisy, each one wrenching from deeper in my gut than the last. A beaming man carrying a blue helium balloon and a packet of tiny white vests passed by and gave me the thumbs up.

I leaned a wet cheek against the cold of the wall, my nightgown tied tightly around my slack belly. My eyes were fixed on the stairwell willing Steve's shape to rise from it.

'Beth, Beth? Are you OK? What are you doing standing here?'

I turned and saw the nurse who had pulled the pin from the grenade the night before. She was wearing her coat; her shift was over. I'd hoped never to see her again.

'At least it's your second child,' she said, over my gulps and judders. 'You've already experienced being a mother. You should be thanking God this didn't happen on your first baby. Can you imagine what it must be like for *those* mothers?'

★ ★ ★

She'd only been an hour old when this nurse, starting her shift, placed Ismae in the Perspex mini-cot beside me and asked if she looked like my other child.

I bristled.

My eyes feigned puzzlement and I nodded at her. 'Of course. Why?'

My head was screaming, *No.*

No, Al doesn't have those almond eyes. No, he doesn't have those chubby fingers. NO, NO, NO.

'Oh. I see. Well, I might get the paediatrician to take a look at her anyway.' She yanked the blue curtains around our half of the room and left.

Steve was quiet, so I knew he was working up to saying something.

'Beth, I think Ismae — Mae, I like how that sounds: Mae? — '

I didn't respond. Caring about her name felt ridiculous now.

'I think Mae might be,' he looked for the least wrong thing to say, 'different, Beth. I'm not sure what I think but my stomach is sick.'

He paused for a moment, putting words around what was staring him in the face. 'It's her eyes. Mostly. She doesn't really look like either of us, you know.' He took my hand.

'It doesn't matter. Whatever it is. It doesn't matter,' I lied.

'No, you're right. It doesn't.' He smiled

58

and squeezed my hand. I knew he meant it and I envied him.

★ ★ ★

A man we both took to be The Paediatrician walked into the room and Steve stood. Dr Burke introduced himself and set about examining our tiny girl. He didn't offer any congratulations and I despised him, right then, in that room, with the passion of a hormonal forty-year-old. When he was finished, he turned to face us. I knew my life would change as soon as he spoke.

'Beth and Steve, I think your daughter may have Down syndrome. I'm very sorry.'

'You *think* she does?' Steve ran his hands through his hair. 'You're not *sure*, then?' His tone was the sort that might precede punching someone in the face.

'If I were a betting man, I wouldn't put my money on her.' He sighed. 'You've been unlucky. A blood test will confirm it but I'm pretty certain.'

'When will you be *absolutely* certain?'

'At a push, I might have results for you next Monday.'

★ ★ ★

I heard my father's imposing voice ask, 'Beth O'Connor?' out in the corridor. I knew his overcoat would be swinging open with his urgent walk.

He was next to me in an instant. Even though he was crying when he gripped me, I thought I felt safer and more capable.

'I'm sorry. It's absurd for me to come in here and let you down.' He pressed his eyes with his handkerchief. Then he bent over and peered in at Ismae.

'She's a beauty, Beth,' he said quietly to his granddaughter's face.

'It's just so very unfair, so unfair. Oh, my darling.' My mother's voice came through the curtain before she did. I hated hearing such disappointment out loud, hearing that little Ismae was a dud. My mother hugged me tightly and looked into my swollen eyes. I saw that hers were swollen too.

After a moment, she joined my father at the giant plastic lunchbox where the faulty baby lay.

'Oh! She's beautiful. Just beautiful.' Her surprise was real. 'I didn't know what to expect, Beth. I'm sorry. I don't know what to say.'

My father picked my sleeping daughter up and, closing his eyes, he pressed his nose to hers. Then he moved her to the crook of his left arm and rocked her, very gently. He could always do things with the appearance of ease.

My mother put her arm around his back and leaned in to admire her granddaughter. 'You are a little dote. Those doctors are fools. We'll show them,' she said.

She turned her face to look at me and dropped her voice: 'Do you want me to call a priest, or something, just in case? I mean, it can't hurt. Miracles happen all the time.'

★   ★   ★

The sounds of cutlery and vacuuming woke me the next morning. The air was warm with the smell of eggs. For a second, I didn't know where I was but I could feel that something was wrong. And then I saw Ismae and the pain started again, picking up where it had left off. She was in my father's arms, the two of them locked in the most exquisite staring match. He was sitting on a chair with his left leg stretched out in front of him. The side of his bad hip. His coat was hung on the chair by its shoulders, the shiny black lining trailing on the marble-look lino floor.

His face was crumpled and his hair stuck out at the back above the stiffness of his white shirt collar.

And I had a memory of being held in his arms myself, in just the same way. I was seven years old and we were sitting on a real marble floor in a holiday complex in Portugal.

I'd been in the building's lift on my own when the steel panelled door had opened a fraction and stopped. A cold and sweaty feeling rose up inside me. With my eye up to the gap, I started to scream. Dropping my bucket of shells, I jammed the second and third fingers of both my hands in between the door and its frame.

I heard my father calling to me, his voice getting louder, the sound of shuffle-running in flip-flops. The tops of his fingers joined me in the lift.

'I'll have you out of there in no time, Beth. Don't worry, angel. Just don't push any buttons.'

I stopped pushing all the buttons. I was queasy with terror but I stopped screaming. I kept my eye up to the gap, where I could see the pocket of his powder-blue shirt.

The door groaned and started to move. Then his entire hands were in the lift with me. Now it was his turn to groan as a triangular gap appeared at the top of the panel, where it was being dragged to one side. His tanned arms reached over and lifted me up and out through it. When my bare feet touched that marble floor, I burst into tears. And he sat down on it with me and held me safely in his arms.

He couldn't make a triangle to get me out of the lift this time, so he was climbing into it with me.

⋆ ⋆ ⋆

There were no windows in Dr Burke's private rooms.

He sat behind a leather-topped desk leafing through a green file with 'Baby O'Connor' written across the top in black marker. A label with a long barcode was stuck under the writing. Steve and I watched his face, watched his hands. The aforementioned 'Baby O'Connor' slept between us, pink-faced and cosy in her car seat. The smell of stale air was suffocating.

These were our last seconds of not knowing with absolute certainty. Yet I willed him to speak, to shout it out, so we could know the worst instead of just fearing it.

Dr Burke made a sucking-in noise before tightening his lips, giving way to a malevolent half-smile, showing no teeth.

Fucking say something.

He nodded to himself at what he was reading, his brows knitted together. I felt my life close in to nothing.

I will shadow this child for all her days.

'Well, it's as I thought.' He'd been right

about not placing that bet. 'Little Baby O'Connor here — '

'Ismae.' Steve interrupted him.

'Yes, Ismae — has Trisomy 21, the most common form of Down syndrome.'

I will never be free.

'The worst thing you can do is go down under this. While I know it's not what anyone wants to hear, you must look at the positives. And there are a couple.'

I tilted my head, begging for anything. Steve sat forward doing the same. Silent tears were running down his face. I saw that he'd missed a patch of stubble over by his ear when he'd shaved this morning for the first time in a week.

'I've examined your daughter thoroughly and I think she's one of the 'good ones'.' He made inverted commas around the last two words with his fingers. He smiled down at her. 'She's alert and she's healthy. Who knows? She might even end up getting a job in a nice café.'

She was six and a half days old.

★   ★   ★

Steve and I sat in a not-nice café opposite the hospital trying to breathe through the black fog that was settling in around us. Our daughter — the future Table Clearer — was snoring now, her car seat up beside me in the booth.

Over the last week, Steve and I had been cemented to each other through the shocking power of shared pain. Supporting each other like two leaning walls, we moved around the house in tandem: together in the kitchen making tea we wouldn't drink; together bathing Mae in the plastic yellow bath that used to be Al's; together saying goodnight to Al and reaching for his light before heading to the next room; a conjoined pair.

'I wish I had a mum to ring. It's silly, I know, but I do.' His voice was quiet as he looked up from staring at the photocopied pages he had been handed by Dr Burke's secretary. She had given him a wide, pitying smile: *You poor man.*

Steve's mother had died when he was nineteen. Immediately my mind turned on itself. What if I died when Mae was nineteen?

I imagined her at a summer fete in a residential unit twenty years from now, manning a stall selling fairy cakes she had baked all by herself. People would pay too much and not take a cake, or maybe just the one, refusing her change, confusing the pricing system it had taken her so long to devise.

He passed the pages to me. Grainy pictures of smiling children looked up from them. Some were wearing glasses, which did little to hide the extra folds around their eyes. I looked at Mae. I was glad she was asleep; eyes closed, tongue in.

I glanced around the café. No one in it struck me as a person I'd want to know. They probably weren't people whose remarks I'd care about anyway.

At the table to my right, a little girl of about four was sitting on a chair swinging her legs. I saw her look at my baby and smile. A woman sat opposite her, obscured by a newspaper. Every now and then, the girl would give a little knock on the pages to remind her she was there. The woman, whom I took to be her mother, must've noticed these little appeals, but she didn't react.

I thought about Steve's colleague Brian and his wife who had called the previous day with champagne. 'When something like this happens, it really makes you appreciate your normal children,' she had said.

The girl to my right began to swing her legs a bit more. And then to tilt her chair backwards onto two legs a little, and then another little bit.

As I saw it totter, I jerked my hand out toward her in a pointless gesture. The chair crashed backwards to the ground, its tubular metal back clanging and echoing around the room. Mae jumped and I panicked that she'd open her eyes and I'd have to put her seat down onto the floor. The girl's face was flushed with embarrassment as she lay in a heap, holding her elbow.

'JESUS CHRIST!' Newspaper pages were slapped in on themselves and the woman jumped to her feet. She grabbed a tiny wrist and yanked the girl up onto her feet.

'JESUS CHRIST!' again.

The girl let out a small cry.

'COME ON. OUT. NOW. And stop bloody whingeing. I'm mortified. You are *SUCH* A RETARD.'

* * *

Since we'd returned home with Ismae, messages from other mothers with 'Down's children' — as my mother called them — were being left on my phone.

I told Steve that there was no point in me contacting these people. Their situations were different. That paediatrician had said that Ismae was one of the 'good ones', which I now interpreted as 'The Best One'. She would be a global marvel, miraculously 'normal' and ordinary.

One bouquet of flowers arrived, a display of simple yellow roses. The card attached said, 'Thinking of you and baby Ismae. Call if you need anything. From Sommer & Rashid (in Number 6).'

I remembered running out of vases, and then out of surfaces to stand makeshift vases on, in the days after we brought Al home from the hospital nearly twelve years before. Steve had opened the windows in our flat to let out the smell of the flowers.

I put the roses on the mahogany table that dominates our unused dining room. I looked out the window at the tidy hedges and the hanging baskets of the two houses opposite. I wondered if anyone was looking back at me right now, if Anna's manicured fingers hooked the sides of the blinds away from the windows while I stood there. I left the room and shut the door.

★   ★   ★

I feared my daughter.

Sometimes when she cried in the night, I worried that her pain marked the onset of a monstrous illness. But then when she slept peacefully for a few hours and didn't cry, I panicked that her unreliable brain had forgotten to waken her to eat.

I didn't know if I could love her. I certainly couldn't love her like I loved Al.

Maybe it wouldn't matter; she wouldn't have the capacity to know the difference.

★　★　★

'You're very lucky, Beth. Your baby is healthy. She has none of those heart problems that they get.'

'And she can hear. She opened her eyes a minute ago when I dropped that plate.'

Anna and Moirah were discussing my good fortune. I smiled tightly.

We were in the sitting room in my house, which Moirah called the reception room. Mae was a month old.

'And they're so loving. And happy.' Moirah was still talking.

'Oh, yes.' Anna had heard this said. 'Down's children are known for their good humour.'

'It could be much worse, Beth. Honestly.' Moirah rested her palms on her pregnant belly. 'You've actually been lucky with Ismae.' I knew she wanted me to see it that way.

The odds of her having a perfect baby were surely increased now. Two babies, born within weeks of each other, in Vesey Hill, with a profound disability? It was unlikely. I'd done her a favour.

'Kate was shocked when I told her because you always eat so well. But I told her it was nothing to do with nutrition. I told her you were chosen to have this baby, because you can do this,' said Anna.

'We only get what we can cope with in this life,' Moirah agreed.

'I'd never be able for it, but then you're stronger than I am.'

Beauty and intelligence were Anna's two favourite qualities in a child. Mae would offend her every day.

'And I do think that of all the disabilities to get landed with, Down's is probably the best one,' Moirah cooed.

'Do you? What makes you say that?' I wanted to revel in the horrors of unthinkable conditions we had escaped.

'Well, you know, them being so happy. And so loving.' She was smiling uncertainly.

'But even so, we're not making light of it. It *is* a shame you didn't have that test when it was offered so you could have made an informed choice. Moirah here has had herself scanned and probed every other week since her first trimester.'

Mae stirred on my lap and yawned in her sleep.

★　★　★

When we went for walks, I stretched the hood of the pram around until it looked like it might tear. I told Steve and Al it was because of the bitter February wind.

Mae's condition had made celebrities of us — the cheap-magazine kind that people want to know all about but would never want to be. I wasn't just another mother walking her baby around the orderly avenues behind the big gates, I was Beth — *Ismae's mum* — you know, *the one with Down's.*

The last word was mouthed, with no sound.

I bumped into Saoirse in the butcher's one Saturday morning. I had left Al and Steve at home dangling plastic Early Learning Centre toys in front of Mae's face. Holding a bag of chops, Saoirse introduced me to her sister by miming rocking a baby while saying my name.

★   ★   ★

Now we were always last on the road to leave for school in the mornings.

I waited until all the other mums' cars had pulled out of their driveways before I opened the front door, Mae in my arms facing into my chest, a blanket around her; Al behind me dragging his bag.

He complained because he liked to get to school early, to sort his locker out and get his books organised for the day. I explained that things were bound to take a bit longer in the mornings with a baby to get ready too.

★ ★ ★

My appearance started to matter to me more than ever before.

Steve was glad to see I was looking after myself, doing what the doctor had said — not going down under this. He seemed to accept his daughter for the beauty she was, for things that he called her 'honesty and purity'.

I put on make-up to sweep the wet leaves from the front garden now. Like the rest of them did. I didn't want to look like the mother of a disabled child.

★ ★ ★

Lying on her back in her basket, Mae raised her arms up straight at me while her mouth quivered at the sides, as though choosing its words. Her almond eyes held mine — *Please don't look away.*

Her lips spread wide and she made her first wholly convincing smile. Her face shone as though lit by a million stars. She made a

72

noise like a giggle. She was six weeks old.

I laughed out loud and lifted her, pressing her body to mine. And, just for those few seconds, I thought the world might hold tiny possibilities.

The Appearance of Coping

'Her back is straight!' Agnes said with surprise.

'Yes. Yes, it is.'

I thought my grandmother must have been confusing her disabilities.

'Well, I'm very happy to see that.'

She was smiling down at Mae, who was sitting on the floor of her playroom, driving a small plastic fire engine over the hills created by her outstretched legs.

'She doesn't have spina bifida, Grandma.'

'Isn't that good news? Well, that's certainly very positive.'

'But nobody thought she had. She has Down — '

'Let's not focus on the negatives. No good comes from that.'

She smoothed her skirt and looked into my face.

'Do you think I could hold her on my lap? Only if you think so — I don't want to upset the little mite.'

'Of course. She'd love that.'

I lifted my daughter — ten months old at the time and sitting very straight, Agnes was quite right — onto her lap, facing in.

For the first three months of her life, visitors had scrutinised Mae's face. They would peer into her basket looking for signs: does she have little folds around her eyes? Are her ears low set? Is there any real definition to her jaw line? Sometimes, they would squint their own eyes and tilt their heads to focus their stares. There was no need for scrutiny once her features got bigger.

My grandmother lived some distance away and hadn't seen her since she'd last visited at the end of March, when Mae was only nine weeks old.

'Hello, my lovely Ismae. You have a very straight back. Like a good lady should have. Perhaps you'll be a champion horse rider.' She kissed her nose. 'And you have the most beautiful eyes.'

Mae reached up and stroked a wrinkly old cheek with her right hand.

'There's nothing wrong with that child.' My mother was carrying a tray with tea and scones from my kitchen. 'She's the brightest button I've ever come across. Without exception.'

Having four generations of her family in the one room had made her excitable. She put the tray down on a side table and set about organising cups and saucers.

'I say it to Dermot all the time. She will buy and sell the rest of them, you mark my words. *Al* will have to keep up with *her*.'

My grandmother and I nodded and smiled because neither of us wanted to disagree.

As my mother went back to the kitchen for cream, my grandmother patted my hand and spoke quietly.

'Ismae will make her own way, Beth. Don't you worry.'

'What in God's name is this dreadful creature?' My mother was back, cream jug in one hand and a blue, fuzzy-haired stuffed toy in the other.

'It's some kind of rodent, I think,' I offered. 'Judging by its teeth and tail.'

'Dear Lord! Is it for Ismae? I can't imagine it appeals to her.'

My mother did a little dance in front of Mae, shaking the rat from side to side to test her theory.

Mae laughed.

The blue rat had arrived in the post from Steve's cousin the previous week.

'*What* is *that?*' Steve had asked, smirking and turning it upside down to look for clues.

'The world's most unsafe baby toy. In blue.' I wanted him to judge it before I said where it was from.

'And it looks like it's been around the

block a few times.' He was frowning.

'It has. It came from the other side of the world. Your cousin Lisa sent it.' I handed him the padded envelope listing her name and address.

'Well, we can comfort ourselves knowing she had to put her hand in her pocket for the postage at least.'

He smiled and put it up on top of a cupboard in the kitchen.

'Another bargain bin toy for Mae,' I said, but he was practising his golf swing with an imaginary club and pretended not to hear.

★   ★   ★

I hadn't fallen in love with Mae right away. My right arm was so taut when I was holding her that it would go numb supporting her tiny weight. I'd held Al the same way for hours when he was a baby without any discomfort. The days I shared with him, when he was brand new, had slid by with ease. With the grating of Steve's key in the door in the evenings, our shared magic seemed to dilute. But with baby Mae, my heart skipped when I saw the boxy lights of our car turning on to the street. I would go toward them, my arms outstretched, ready to hand her over.

Steve would take her from me and I would

walk away from him, from her, shut the bedroom door behind me, shut myself down to all of it and sleep.

She could be very noisy, noisier than I ever remembered Al being. Some days when she was teething, she would cry almost incessantly, pausing for a moment only to draw a breath and rev up again.

Al bought her a little brown bear with some of his birthday money, 'to cheer you up,' he said, in the high-pitched voice he adopted to talk to his adored little sister. He spoke more loudly that day, so she might hear him over her tight-fisted squeals. He knelt down so his face was to her face. Mae looked into his eyes and then batted the bear aside with her left arm and continued to wail.

Al looked at the bear lying on its back in a fitted tartan jacket and he frowned.

'Maybe I should have just bought the pink one.'

He looked up at me, his voice small.

'But I thought the brown one was cool, you know? That she might like a break from all the pink stuff.'

My chest hurt for him. And for a moment, I hated her. I imagined him, an older man, trying to please a sister whose feelings and thoughts he might never understand.

★   ★   ★

When we were out for our Saturday morning walk that weekend, I told Steve how I couldn't bear to think of Al's life restricted when we were gone and Mae little more than an adult baby.

'Jesus, Beth. I don't want to hear it. I can't hear it.' He sounded weary.

'Don't you ever feel like it's too much to cope with? Like she is too much to cope with?'

Steve sighed. 'Stop, Beth. You've had months to get your head around this.'

'Well, I'm sorry but I haven't,' I snapped. 'I don't know if I can. Everyone is assuming I can, even you. Just expecting me to get on with it. To just keep going.'

'Well, what else is there, Beth? What else can we do?'

'But don't you wish it was — *different?*' I pushed. 'That she was different?'

'Don't I wish she was *the same*, you mean? That's what you're really asking me.' His tone was sharp now. 'And, yes, I suppose I do. I wish she was Mae, but without Down syndrome. Does it make you feel better to hear me say that?'

'No, because it's ridiculous. Then she wouldn't be Mae, would she?'

79

'I don't know — would she? I *don't know* what I mean, Beth. And that's the truth.' He stopped walking and looked at me, his eyes looking for something in mine. 'I just want her to be her, to be my Mae. But without the worry. And without the fear.'

'You want her to be normal.'

He rubbed his free hand across his brow and then down over his face and said nothing more.

'Well, that's never going to happen.' I think I said this out loud but I can't be sure. And there was no reaction to it if I did.

We walked on, holding hands in the tense silence. Looking in opposite directions, veering apart.

★   ★   ★

But we did our best. Made an effort to reclaim ourselves.

We even planned a trip to Paris. Just the two of us for Steve's birthday. He had never been. Mae was nearly a year old and the sting of those early weeks was giving way to a more subdued resignation.

We sat side by side on the plane, new magazines in front of us, sunglasses on our heads. Like before, in a way. Just a couple going away for the weekend.

Three days away together, just Steve and me. Without Al and Mae. I'd see them again, see *her* again, in three days. Two nights only. Not long at all.

I looked around at things, tried to take them in, tried carefully to enjoy myself. I watched little baggage trucks outside circle around, stop, circle around, stop. The sky was cloudy. I turned my head away from the window, from the grey.

A smell of new plastic filled the aisle. Overhead bins were being crammed full and slammed shut. I watched passengers file in, glancing at their tickets, counting ahead to find their seats to see who they were next to, to see if they would have enough space for their bags, for themselves. Before the doors were locked.

As I fastened my seat belt, the possibility of death crept into my lap with the buckle, a sinister animal, curling around me. Strapped in, I felt constricted, felt something clawing. I stretched out my legs and breathed in. But the animal tightened itself around my ribs.

What if the plane went down with both of us on it? Killing Steve and me. Orphaning Al. *Orphaning Mae.*

Something pushed its might against me in the seat.

Who would take care of her if we were both

gone? Who would love her?

I got off the plane, so Steve had to follow me.

We didn't go to Paris.

We didn't go away together, like before. We weren't just a couple, like before. We went home together, diluted a little further.

Happy birthday to you.

★   ★   ★

Steve did all the flying since, alone, for work.

I focused instead on getting a routine going at home. Routine would make those occasional waves of messy, uneven sadness more manageable. Routine would protect the family unit. So everyone had said. The appearance of coping can be part of the coping. So they said.

I made time to shave my legs and *not let myself go*. Another thing that people said was important.

I still played the 'Which Disability Is Worse?' game in my head, but I was definitely doing it less. Only really in the car now, if I was stuck in traffic. Mostly, I settled on autism or blindness. I remembered a primary school teacher I'd had who was fond of saying, *There's always someone worse off than yourself*. I thought of her now and then and wondered what other helpful clichés she might know.

And I still found myself expecting the worst. I still dwelt on the risks of things, still anticipated loss a lot of the time. But I tried to keep my mind busy, to keep it from idling on the challenges ahead. Like people suggested.

If I could avoid it at all, I didn't go to the supermarket with Mae, though. I hated her being up so high in the trolley, nearer eye level. I hated the second glances, the third glances, and maybe then sometimes even a pat on her head and a pitying smile at me.

I met two mothers from Al's school there one Thursday.

'She actually looks like Al, doesn't she?' Claire had said. 'I mean that in a good way. For her,' she went on. 'And for Al too, of course,' tangling herself up.

'Well, he is her brother.' I smiled. 'I'd expect there to be some family resemblance.' I think I kept my voice light.

They nodded and exchanged a look that one might describe as Significant.

Square Pegs

'This could be our new place, Mae. Our group,' I told her as I parked outside the Mother and Toddler Group (Special Needs). She was almost two years old and we were both in the market for some friends.

She stopped making handprints in the condensation on the window and clapped, as though she understood.

The group met in a room at the back of the parish centre and from the poster I'd gathered that there was no particular leader or facilitator — 'Run by Mums', it said.

Inside, little chairs made three stacked towers against the wall. They were plastic, but friendly looking; bright and chunky and ample. Not the mean steel and pinchy brown ones that I'd feared. The women were glossy and notably well-turned-out for a toddler morning. I wondered if they'd always taken this level of care or if we'd all undergone the same kind of change after these children were born.

We sat in a close circle: mothers at the back, each child sitting to the front on the hard cushion created by familiar crossed legs.

Until now, when Mae was in a room people hadn't seemed to notice the other children, their watchful eyes casually returning to her again and again. Here, for the first time, she was not being paid undue attention. Is this where she actually fit in? Among these children with visible disabilities, misshapen limbs, hearing aids and leg splints?

We sang a little song to welcome the children to the group.

Obedient and gentle, they played with their hands or small toys for the duration; a little boy with cerebral palsy leaned sideways into the warmth of his mother's chest, lost in his own thoughts.

I could see now that these children were largely unreadable.

The introductions and welcomes over, the women's voices lost their sing-song and so did the conversation. Things like how to keep your whites white without over-washing were discussed. One said that the key was to turn your washing line *toward the sun*. The woman beside her then asked precise questions about this. Another said nothing but looked out at the sunshine, considering the plausibility of it.

I smiled to myself thinking of a conversation Sommer and I had the day before.

'You really need to get your act together,

ironing-wise,' she'd said.

'Excuse me?'

'If you must do it yourself, you really need to stay on top of it. Your basket is almost full. Whatever would Moirah think, if she saw this chaos. Tsk.'

'You know, you can be quite a cow,' I said. 'For a Muslim.'

'A halal cow.'

★ ★ ★

'Do you like them?' A voice beside me was asking me a question, directly.

'I'm sorry?'

'My earrings. I noticed you looking at them.'

I hadn't been, but I did now.

The talking around me stopped; the circle was too close to allow for several conversations at once. Faces looked from my face to the earrings and back again.

'They catch your eye, don't they?'

'Yes, they do,' I supposed.

The faces waited for their opportunity to jump in.

And she gave them one. 'They were far too expensive, but I couldn't help it. We deserve nice things, don't we? Heaven knows, we've enough on our plates.'

She tilted her head and, with a wide-eyed pantomime nod in the direction of the child on her lap, she encouraged me to relate to her.

And then they were off, exchanging nods and agreements. And it all felt uncomfortably familiar.

I looked across at my daughter, who had wriggled out of my crossed legs within seconds of being put there. She was humming and spinning in a circle, her arms stretched high above her head. She got dizzy and lost her balance. Toppling over, she plopped onto her nappy and laughed loudly, her mouth open wide. Raw and alive, she saw me watching and her expression settled into a huge smile. Her love was naked, written on her face.

I started to hope that I was wrong. That Mae and I didn't actually belong here.

For the rest of the hour, we did our best to join in. On short breaks between spinning, Mae sat on my lap and hummed 'Twinkle Twinkle' while I alternately 'Contributed To' and 'Showed Interest In' the topics of the morning. When things went quiet for a moment, I mentioned that I had recently shopped around for a weight-based deal on my refuse collection. Which was not a total lie, being something that I did mean to do. Whenever.

We stayed until the end. The little chairs

stayed in their towers.

Seeing me reach for my jacket, Mae ran to her buggy by the wall and wheeled it to the door. Once she had clambered in — all chubby legs and effort — she set about securing the harness at her lap with determined fingers.

When we got into our car outside, we squeezed each other and shared a conspiratorial giggle.

'If you don't mind, I think we'll give our group a miss next week, Mae,' I said, as I fastened her seat belt. She took off her new hair band and shook her long hair out. Examining it for a moment, she flung the band onto the floor and burrowed back into her car seat and shut her eyes.

As I reversed out of the parking space, I thought about telling Steve about it and how we didn't plan to go again. But I'd need to phrase it so he wouldn't see it as another example of me 'not accepting our reality'.

I'd ask Sommer what to do. A Muslim woman renting in Vesey Hill, she'd know a thing or two about survival.

Starfish

The first time I'd seen Steve's car, I whistled.

A dark blue lounge-on-wheels was parked outside my house.

He'd announced that it was a Chrysler Valiant VG. That it previously had something called a Slant 6 engine in it but that he'd replaced it with something called a V8. 'Years ago now.' He nodded while he spoke, happy with the change.

'Good thinking,' I said.

I loved how tiny I felt next to him on the long single front seat of the Valiant.

'You should know you'll always come second to this car.' He smiled.

'But of course.'

★   ★   ★

I wasn't surprised to find myself falling for him. He pursued me with a gentle, charming persistence — showing up week after week, calling every other day, bringing little gifts. His arms around me always warm and solid.

He bought me an answering machine after our first month together, so he could leave messages for me to come home to — one, two, sometimes three or four in a row.

'You can close your eyes and it'll be like I'm right here already annoying you as soon as you get in.'

The next day I came home to a blinking light on the coffee table beside the dusty, unread book on Degas.

Beep.

'It's me.' He was laughing already, at his own joke, before he told it. I loved that.

'How do you turn a duck into a jazz musician?'

The sound of the receiver being hung up.

Beep.

'Put it in the microwave until its Bill Withers.' Laughter. Like it was the first time he'd heard it himself.

★   ★   ★

I knew that his last girlfriend had had sensitive ears because he spent much of our first couple of months together trying to get the desired reaction out of mine. But then he came to know my body, every inch of it, like nobody had before.

And I knew things with him were different, that I was different: I didn't find myself smiling at other men; I didn't mention it if they smiled at me. I didn't want to unsettle him. I wanted to protect him. To love him.

When we bought our first bed together — a Super King-sized ocean of cotton — we would lie on our backs holding hands, trying to cover each corner of the bed, looking at the white plaster ceiling, silent; two starfish.

★ ★ ★

This morning Steve was in the kitchen when I came down. He was leaning over the sink eating a slice of toast, avoiding my eyes under the pretence of keeping crumbs from falling onto the floor.

'Hi.'

No answer.

'Hi,' I said again, louder now. As if him not hearing was why he hadn't replied.

'Oh, hi.' He opened a press and shut it again, busying himself about nothing.

His shirt collar was folded into his jumper on one side, but I didn't tell him.

After a moment, he slid the back door across and a breeze blew in. He set about moving the trampoline and the mock-Tudor playhouse so he could mow the lawn.

As I watched him, I could see my own reflection in the glass and I was confronted with just how old I looked when I was frowning.

* * *

'Look what I have for you, darling.' Moirah had called at the door and was in the kitchen talking to Mae by the time Steve came back in.

She was holding a pair of pink *Hello Kitty* sunglasses out toward her.

'I thought of you the moment I saw these so I just had to buy them.'

Mae beamed and walked toward them, shyly.

'Sunglasses, just for you.'

Mae took them and ran to my lap to show me.

'Mae's pink glasses,' I said clearly, making oval shapes around my eyes with my hands.

She grinned and put them up to her eyes.

I fixed their weight on her tiny ears and lifted her up to the mirror so she could see herself.

'Beau-ti-ful,' I said, separating the syllables so she had time to take each of them in.

'Oh, you look GORGEOUS, Mae!' Moirah said.

Mae giggled and patted her chest with both her hands the way she did when she felt she looked good.

'Mine,' she said. 'Nice.'

'Yes, that's right. Nice. Good girl,' Steve

said, smiling. 'My darling.'

'Quick, Beth! Take a photo of her wearing them! Before she takes them off. Go on, *quick!* Standing there, with them on, you'd never even know, would you, Steve?'

He turned so his back was to Moirah, to her ugly words. He kissed our daughter's forehead and left the room. I heard the front door shut behind him a moment later.

I went upstairs and looked out the bedroom window. He drove a silver Audi now but he wasn't taking it. I watched him cross the street, head down, hands thrust into his pockets. From here, he looked like any other moody middle-aged man shambling along.

He manoeuvred around a skip which was sitting up on the clipped green verge opposite. A drawer sat on top of other discarded furniture; its front was finished in pine but the sides normally hidden from view were a cheap white plastic.

★   ★   ★

Now, in the sitting room, I looked at the lamp he had given me for my last birthday and wondered when we'd become so deadened. When we'd started undressing with our backs to each other. I'd been pained and angry for months now, his life having returned to its normality and importance soon after Mae's birth while mine stayed still, stuck. He had allowed my anger, never wanting to tackle it, leaving it to hang in the air unchecked, gradually making him distant and then resentful. It was easier now to live through our days separately, with pain and distance, together apart in this big brash house.

He and Al were on the other couch, Steve staring at the television while Al slept against his shoulder. Because Steve hadn't lifted his arm, Al looked like a child who had fallen asleep on a plane and dropped against a stranger who was unsure quite what to do about it.

I took a bite of one of the cheap jelly sweets a neighbour had given Mae and regretted it as soon as its sickly mess coated my teeth.

'Do you want to lift your arm and let him in?' I said, my eyes down on the book in my lap.

'No.' The answer was short and sudden, like the bite of a glasses case shutting.

I turned the page even though I hadn't read any of the words.

'I'll carry him up.' His voice came a little softer, looking at Al.

And then, 'I won't be back down.'

As Steve stood trying to gather the mass of our son's long limbs in his arms, the newspaper fell from the folds of Al's lap. When I picked it up, I saw that he had drawn neat boxes in red pen around the programmes he wanted to watch. And had written 'MUM' and 'DAD' in different colours over the ones he thought myself or Steve might enjoy. Our lives in colour-coded boxes. And none of them the same.

My Piano

'Mind you don't sit on the treat!' Marion said urgently.

I stopped, knees bent, and turned to see that I was about to lower myself onto a mini Crunchie that lay on the chair.

'Oh. I'm sorry,' I said, picking it up and moving to place it on her desk next to the sign that assured me that she was in fact the Senior Speech and Language Therapist.

'No, no. It's for you. It's something I like to do when I'm meeting new parents of the service for the first time. I find it's a nice ice-breaker.'

'I see. Thank you.'

Holding the bar in my hand, I sat back into the chair.

'Ordinarily, I would have a parent of another child here on the first morning too.' She motioned at the chair to my right which had a mini Bounty on it. 'I like to meet new people in twos. I think it can be very helpful for parents going through the same things to bounce ideas off each other.' She paused. 'But the other lady called to cancel a little earlier.' She shrugged, and in raising her

96

shoulders and eyebrows together she let me know that *you couldn't be up to some people*.

Her black woollen top was dotted with the little fur balls of age and, as she stretched awkwardly across her desk to retrieve the Bounty, I saw that the back of it was covered in long white dog hairs.

'As it's just the two of us, I'll get cracking straight away and show you this DVD. It's an overview of the main points I will be covering when I start my series of home visits to you and Ismae next week.'

'OK, yes. Thank you.'

Marion turned her laptop toward me and a slide show began. The fact that we were opposite each other meant she now had nothing to look at but my face, which was looking at the screen. This had the effect of causing me to overdo my reactions; nodding sagely at common-sense tips, smiling when a cute child appeared, frowning in a villainous way at the list of Things Not to Do — speak with your back to the child, speak too quickly — and the accompanying illustrations with the big red Xs through them. Every so often I would look up and meet her eyes and we would nod together, two women on the same wavelength.

The presentation ambled along to the

strains of forgettable string music for almost twenty-five minutes, by which time the foil-covered Crunchie sat damp in my palm.

'So, what did you think?' She beamed.

'Yes, very informative. I understand how young children would benefit from hearing short, clear phrases.' I quoted the DVD back at her.

'Exactly. And particularly children like Ismae. I see she's twenty-six months old now. As you know, sign language is absolutely key for these children. Does she sign much?'

'Not really. She signs for 'bedtime' and 'love' and . . . ' I tried to think of any other gestures she made in the normal run of things that might be construed as signing.

I'd lost interest in signing shortly after our first few attempts at it. Steve and I both found the manuals' insistence on Waiting for a Sign before granting our little girl anything or before doing anything for her to be peculiar and unnatural. Mae communicated beautifully with us through touch, sound, and single words. Shelving the signing books, we agreed that she would speak in her own time.

Lately she had started to draw balls and circles with her chunky crayons and would point with confidence and say 'Baawl' to rapturous applause. Then she would trot triumphantly over to me, climb up, and burrow into my lap. And we would bask in each other like two cats in the sun.

'She does have quite a few single words though. I know she'll get there,' I said, wondering if I actually did.

Marion frowned a little but snapped out of it with a dramatic, 'Well, she's still young. We will have her signing in no time! I'll come to your home at four next Monday to see you and Mae in your own *environs*. I'll be able to show you how to play and we can look at how you might be playing wrong.'

Playing wrong.

I questioned myself again now. Why was I humouring this? When had I become so obedient?

We said our goodbyes and I left, the Crunchie melting in my clenched hand.

★ ★ ★

My daughter played hide and seek with Marion that scheduled Monday, the former doing all the hiding, the latter failing at seeking.

Mae collapsed her body into tiny spaces down on the floor behind various chairs, her knees pressed into her cheek sockets, her chubby arms holding all of her together, her wrists bent so that her hands were over her ears. If

she couldn't hear herself giggling, then neither could that annoying lady with the lipstick
on her teeth and the crazy, exaggerated smile
and the sing-song voice and the swooping
arm gestures and the bag of coloured socks to
pair and shapes to match and all kinds of
WAITING and questions about this and that.

Marion was still waving and calling out to
me half an hour after she'd arrived.

'HE-LLO MA-MA!' she sang and signed.
Every time, she would instruct me to
reciprocate by nodding and narrowing her
eyebrows at me.

'HE-LLO MAR-I-ON!' I sang back, giving
a robotic wave.

Mae laughed, her squeezed-shut eyes
making tiny puckered half-moons.

* * *

Her speech, when it came, was something
soft and beautiful; her words without
sharpness had soft edges, were furry almost;
her phrases easy to make out if you stopped
to listen. I was reminded of the muffled
melody of the piano in my mother's house
being played from underneath, the keys
touching green felt when I sat on the floor by
the legs of the stool, my little hand reaching
into the wood from below.

*   *   *

'I love you,' I said as I tucked her into bed every night.

'Aa luvoo thoo,' she said one night, out of the darkness. She was two years and seven months old.

Our first complete, natural and fully spoken conversation. And when I heard it, I knew I'd have waited forever for it.

Suffering Fools

'I'm getting married!' the voice on the phone announced.

'That's great news,' I said, no idea who I was answering.

'Oh, Beth! Beth O'Connor. You don't know who this is, do you?' The voice laughed loudly.

'Sorry, no — '

'It's Victoria!'

'Victoria.' I could only think of one. 'Victoria Hall?'

'Yes! Who else? It's so good to talk to you. I got your number from the phone book. You're in the 01 directory! I couldn't believe it might be you — I thought you'd be living in Berlin or somewhere interesting.'

'Me too! How are you, Victoria?'

'Well, I'm getting married! Can you credit that? Me. Getting married. Ha!'

I thought I'd heard she was already married, years ago. 'I'm delighted for you.'

'And I'm delighted to find *you* because you MUST come. To the wedding. It just wouldn't be the same without you.'

The same as what? I thought, but instead

my mother in me said, 'That's very kind.'

'I'm spending wildly from the bridal purse, as it were,' she trilled, 'and would love to treat you and your husband. You must come. A fabulous weekend away, on me!'

'An entire weekend! That's far too much.'

'You're welcome!' She gave a small cough and her voice became low and confidential. 'I can't tell you how delighted I am that we've picked up where we left off. Honestly, Beth.'

I wasn't quite sure what friendship she was recalling but I knew enough to know that I should say something of note now.

'I'm really glad you called, Victoria.'

'It means a lot for me to have you there for the most important day of my life.'

She made it sound like she meant it.

⋆   ⋆   ⋆

I hadn't seen Victoria since we'd left university over two decades ago. I tried to remember specifics of any time I'd spent with her back then. I came up with one weekend at a literary workshop in Galway when she placed her hand down on my crossed knee in a circle of poets to stop me hopping it. I used to do that when something really captivated me and I forgot myself.

I thought about my own wedding day and

never thinking to invite her. Never thinking of her enough even to forget her. The first thing I did remember about that day was my father telling Steve and me how happy he was to pay for it all. How he had always vowed to give his one child everything. And how he always had. And how we weren't to thank him for paying for it because he liked doing it.

'Anyway, Steve, it makes sense because I have more than you have.'

★   ★   ★

The bride and groom kissed and stood hand-in-hand looking out from the altar so we could bestow our approval.

The reception was a pastel fairy-tale of pashminas and fascinators in a stately restored barn-turned-more-upmarket-barn, a clever seating plan corralling 260 guests.

Even the chairs had made the effort and were wearing gold drapey covers. There were several string quartets and everywhere heady flowers and silver trays. Silver trays for tiny foods and giant drinks. And Victoria gliding through it all, laughing and clasping her hands to her chest each time she was given a compliment or a slim envelope.

With the exception of one woman whose face seemed familiar, I didn't think I'd ever met any of these people before. Who were they? How had Victoria accumulated so many guests? Maybe she had a gift for companionship, for *sociability*, that I lacked. Sitting there, I felt joyless and wizened.

But we'd had friends in London, Steve and I. We did. A good circle of them. And although every year after Christmas some would leave to return home to Ireland and other countries, they had been replaced by others who arrived to start a new year, a new life. So the circle held. It never lost its numbers or its shape. But all that was before we came back to Dublin, to Vesey Hill and the gates that kept the rest of the world out. Which seemed to be what Anna and Moirah liked about them. Behind those gates, they were big fish with big mouths commanding shallow waters.

Sommer was the only person I could think of that I laughed with anymore.

'Was our wedding like this?' I asked Steve as he sat down and handed me a bellini in a cut-crystal glass.

'Nope.'

Across the barn, a man with a moustache and talkative hands was trying to kiss Victoria on the mouth.

'I mean the extravagance, all this *show.*'

'Nope.' He sat back in his chair and was

silent for a moment. 'I loved that day.' He smiled but there was a sad sigh in his voice. 'God, I felt so lucky.'

'So did I.'

It was true. I remembered feeling a real and pure happiness. And feeling it again when I took a book from a shelf a few months later and found grains of sand inside in a line down the centre, brought home from that week in Spain.

But the onslaught of the past years meant it was a long time since either of us had felt particularly lucky. We were losing ourselves, losing each other, in responsibility. How unrecognisable we had become. We might easily now pass one another on the street.

Occasionally, I'd notice Steve trying to make conversation with me, my own husband trying to think of something to say. And I'd feel furious that things had come to this. Furious that he recognised we'd lost our friendship, our sex. It annoyed me that he knew we were so far removed from each other, knew that I felt so far removed from him as a man, as my man, that he was trying to talk about something that might interest me. And I'd feel embarrassed. And I'd want him to just *leave it alone*. So I wouldn't respond right — or at all — and his efforts would dissolve and leave an exhausted silence in their place.

'Ours was definitely a great day — fun, you know,' he said. 'Although I think your mum looked a bit tense for much of it. But that was something to do with your dad. Not the wedding.'

I thought of my father scraping his chair back across the terracotta tiles, causing a loud and jarring noise to bounce off the chalky Spanish walls. I remembered my mother making an attempt at running after him, her arms out on both sides to offset the imbalance caused by her strappy heels.

And him back in his seat later, sitting with his palms together, fingers splayed, his elbows on the table, regarding my mother while she spoke. I remember thinking that his eyes could be quite mean. Then he sat forward, took a handful of olives from a bowl, and threw them into the back of his mouth.

She had started into a story about meeting a teacher in the village who told her that a third of all the children in it were what my mother called 'non-nationals'. She described the teacher at length, trying to recall the colour of her dress — 'maybe it was green, or a kind of a blue, with some sort of a pattern, a diamond maybe' — struggling over the detail, placing huge importance on getting it right.

And I wondered now if this is what

becomes of a woman who loses herself. Who loses her identity. If the power to discern what matters and what's meaningless somehow deserts her. Is this the danger up ahead for women foolish enough to lose their footing in their own lives?

Is this me?

I remember how I watched my father continue to look at her like he was questioning his choice, trying to remember the potential he saw in her. I wondered if he was recalling the poems she might once have inspired. He saw me watching him and he gave me a quick smile, before turning away and throwing more olives down his neck.

Later, when it got dark, he sang 'Brown Eyed Girl', the way he always did when he was pushed to sing something. And I wondered, not for the first time, if it ever bothered my mother because her eyes are blue.

★　★　★

But I could never ask her. It's been a long time since she and I have said anything of real substance to each other. She's so contained, so ferocious in her reserve. What I know of her I know through the little things: the way she stands when my father enters the room;

the way she looks at his face and away down to the floor — up and down, like a hen feeding — seeking something from him when he speaks, when he notices her there. Something that he can never give.

When I was a child, his mood dominated how we lived, how our days would be. When he was relaxed and jovial, we all felt it, were carried along on it. For my mother, it's still the same. But then, I only know the parent versions of their selves, the sides that they let me see.

Mae is our family's barometer for emotion. Like a weather vane, she picks up changes in the atmosphere, feels them keenly, and turns to face them. In an instant, she reads people and the atmosphere in a room and will seek out the discomfort and the pain to confront it. Uncripple it. She looks into my face smiling her widest smile, our noses tipping. And she stays there until I do it back — a real smile. My mouth just making the shape never fools her. She needs to feel the smile, feel my comfort. And it works; my cloud lifts for a time and I do feel it. The appearance of coping is part of the coping.

And now she does it to my mother.

* * *

I remembered something else my father said to me on my wedding day in Spain.

'Marriage is one day at a time, Bethy. Nobody can know for sure that it will last. And nobody can make promises, even though today you feel that you can. Don't set the bar too high or you will disappoint each other.'

I thought that he was cynical, that he was wrong — that I could make promises to myself, to Steve. That we would always put each other first, take on whatever life laid before us and see it through. I didn't realise how much more he knew.

★ ★ ★

I will bump into Victoria on the street four years later and she will be delighted about it, thrilled to see me again. And I will see that she does mean it.

Her husband will be there too and he will make a caustic remark at her. And I'll be sorry to have heard it.

There will be what seems like a long, lifeless silence before she will turn to him and say, 'Let's not argue,' in a weary voice that tells me they usually do.

An Ordinary Face

I was staring into the fridge mulling over options for lunch when my mother rang.

'*There* you are, darling,' she said with relief as though she'd been looking high and low.

'Julie Brooks — you remember Julie, our old neighbour? Well, she rang last night to tell me about a documentary she watched on new cosmetic surgeries. In America.'

'Oh, yes?' I said, checking the date on a forgotten Parmesan wedge.

'She knows about Ismae, you see, and,' her voice grew excited, 'apparently people with Down syndrome can have the extra fold around their eyes taken away and the shape corrected. Now. In America.'

I could hear her clattering around the kitchen while she spoke, opening, closing, emptying, filling, putting away. Even though it was only her and my father in the house and the cleaner came three times a week, she was forever washing and ironing, walking through rooms laden down with folded towels and an empty cup hooked on a finger.

'Pardon?'

'Isn't that wonderful? You can get her eyes

fixed. You just have to take her to America.'

I shut the fridge door.

'Mum, there's nothing wrong with Mae's eyes.'

'I know her *sight* is fine, darling, but I mean the shape. Those little folds.'

I spoke slowly and clearly.

'Mae will not be having cosmetic surgery so we can pretend she doesn't have Down syndrome.'

'Ismae is so pretty, Beth, and clever; she might benefit from being given this chance.'

'No. I don't think she would. But thank Mrs Brooks for her interest.'

'Well, I'll leave the idea with you.' She sighed. 'That's not why I phoned anyway. Are you popping down to me later?'

'I hadn't planned to.' I paused. 'But I can.'

'That would be nice. I wonder if you might remember to bring back my casserole dish when you're coming. And I wanted to talk to you about a fundraiser the golf club are having next month. I went there this morning to meet Orla about it. She had brought along her new *man friend*.'

Her tone suggested this man was bringing something far steamier than friendship to Orla's life.

'Did you want me to do something? For the fundraiser?'

'Well, as it's for Down syndrome, we thought it would be nice to have a few Down's children there, and maybe even some adults — if we thought we could manage them. You know, keep them happy but *under control*. It all depends on how many we can get. Between the ten of us on the committee, we actually only know a few but if each of us got even *one*, let's say, that would be marvellous. So obviously I was thinking that you could bring Ismae, as my one.'

I thought of the group of adults with Down syndrome I'd seen being chaperoned into the circus a few months before. Was that how it went? Sufficient numbers of people with an extra chromosome needed to be rounded up before an outing could be arranged.

'Oh, imagine if we somehow got eighteen of them!' Her voice filled with delight. 'We could assign each of them to a different hole! You know, name a hole after them for the day. Although that's probably far too — '

'I don't rent my daughter out for functions, Mum.'

'But you'd both enjoy it! And she's such a wonderful ambassador for the *condition*.'

I could hear that she'd used this phrase before and I wanted to bang my head off the table.

'Mae is three years old.'

She sighed dramatically to assure me I was being difficult.

'I can talk to you about it later. I'll be here until about five.'

'Fine.'

'OK so.'

'Yes, fine.'

I put the phone down.

★ ★ ★

I pulled up at my parents' house. Al jumped out of the car and ran straight around the side to find a basketball so he could shoot hoops into the net out the back. The sky was pencil grey and the air thick but the rain was holding off.

The front door was unlocked and, as I went into the kitchen, I saw Al pass the window and wave in at my mother. She blew him a kiss and smiled, although for a second I saw her scowl at his skull and crossbones T-shirt.

'Good girl, thank you,' she said as I put her casserole dish into the press above the oven.

I noted again how steady and silently her cupboards closed and clicked by themselves no matter how heavy-handed a slam I might give them.

She was wearing her usual black apron

with Dijon Vu written on it in large, yellow lettering. In smaller letters below, it said, 'the feeling that you've had this mustard somewhere before'. She was spacing out cloves on a side of ham, her eyes focused on her work.

'I didn't mean to upset you earlier, Beth. And you know that I absolutely adore Ismae.'

'I know you do.'

'Lovely.' Her voice brightened. 'So the fundraiser is on the fifteenth of next month — a Friday — so if you could be there with her just before lunch time? We're planning to gather them all by 1.30 and then there will be photos at about 2.'

'She won't be going.'

My mother shook her head slightly.

'I speak up for that child all of the time,' she said, a quiver in her voice. 'And this is just one thing I want you to do for me.'

'Mae doesn't need you to *speak up* for her. And when? With whom?'

'Well, when Janine at the club said that the fabulous little Prada coat your father bought Ismae was very expensive *for her*, I was absolutely livid.'

She swallowed noisily and I saw her hands were unsteady settling the cloves, but she kept her eyes down.

'Jesus fucking Christ.'

'Beth. I won't have you speaking like a

fishwife in my house, whatever the reason. I've just asked you to bring my granddaughter along to an event that — ' Her cheeks were flushed now.

'Mae is not a prop to be paraded around the place so people will feel sorry for her and part with their money.'

She had stopped with the cloves and just stood, looking down, saying nothing.

'You just don't get it, Mum.'

The room was quiet but for the rhythmic sound of Al's basketball thumping the ground in the distance.

And then my gaze came to rest on her fridge door and I felt an unexpected wildness building inside me.

'And why the fuck do you still have that beefeater magnet stuck on your fridge? Can I ask you that, after all this time?'

Every part of me was raging at her now, at the golf club, at Julie Brooks and Janine and the *Prada* coat, at the past, at the whole lot of it.

My words snagged in the space between us and her shocked eyes followed mine, widening further when they settled on the fridge as though seeing the offending little plastic souvenir for the first time.

'This one?' she asked, half-pointing and making things worse. 'Because you bought it for me,' she added quickly. 'You remember? Back from London.'

'*I know* I bought it. It and some bloody shortbread. Of course I remember!' I might have been roaring. 'I bought it in an airport in London before I boarded a plane home because I needed to bring something back to make it look like I had done more that day than just have an abortion.'

Her face was flushed red now. 'I can see how you might feel. I forgot it was there really.' She was chewing on her lipsticked mouth.

'It has been stuck to that fridge for twenty-six years,' my voice was ragged, 'and yet you have never once mentioned it, mentioned anything about that day, not since I stepped through the front door bleeding and dying inside.'

She winced at my words. 'I didn't like to upset you.'

'Christ almighty! You had already upset me. And you left me upstairs in my bed like it was the fucking 1950s.'

And now it was out, unleashed and coursing through the kitchen, knocking over and banging off civilised things — a gleaming cafetière; a column of cookery books; an unused porcelain milk jug. The whole room which was cluttered with shiny nonsense was

117

tainted now, tainted with something real and living.

'Your father would never have coped, Beth. With you having a baby or with you terminating the . . . He'd never have coped. I was trying to protect him.' Her voice was rising to match mine.

'So you sent me for an abortion to spare my father's feelings? And never thought to mention it again?'

Something was climbing up from my stomach, a cold liquid that felt like a power; relief shot through with fear.

'You had plenty to say on it *before* you sent me.'

'You have to try to understand, darling — ' she started.

'No. I don't. I was practically a child myself, your child, and you left me to deal with this huge — '

'I put a tray at your bedroom door that next day, after — but you didn't touch it,' she said. 'So I left you be. Beth, it was for the best.'

'Please stop. Stop with the meaningless clichés.'

She didn't say anything.

'You have always tried to tidy life away. And IT DOESN'T WORK. Surely even you can see that by now?'

She grasped for words to use and, finding none, left the room quickly, as though she'd wrapped the conversation up and was taking it with her to bury it somewhere else.

She came back a moment later and stood in front of me, my rage no longer pinning her to the other side of the room.

'I honestly don't think you would have coped, Beth. And I know your father wouldn't have. I know him like the back of my hand.'

I closed my eyes for a moment, waiting to hear something real from her.

'I was trying to keep things together, us together.'

I didn't know whether she meant her and Dad or me and her.

'And it's not always easy. People make mistakes.'

And on she went, wading through a marsh of overused expressions.

When her words trailed off, I opened my eyes and watched her lean over and peel the faded magnet from the fridge and put it into her pocket beneath the stiff and silly apron. Then she moved forward and lifted her arms out to embrace me.

I stood rigid and silent.

'Sometimes there just isn't enough strength to keep everything together, you know,' I heard myself say over her shoulder.

'I know exactly,' she said.

And I was surprised because I could hear that she did.

* * *

Standing there, I thought about how I'd felt sick when I saw James years later, this boy from my past, laughing across the room at a party; grown up and living his life, nothing holding him back. I remembered how I'd leaned into Steve's frame and linked his arm. I rose up onto my tippy toes. 'Hey there. Can we go?' quietly into his ear.

'There's an old boyfriend of mine here and I'd rather not stay. But only if you don't mind?'

He put his arm around my waist and pulled my body in close. I felt his smile come to my face.

'I'd rather be the only person in the room to have slept with you, so let's get out of here.'

I grinned up at him so he couldn't have guessed how nauseous I was feeling.

* * *

'I saw James, Mum. Years later, when I was first going out with Steve.'

'You didn't mention anything about it, did you?' She pulled back to look at my face.

'No.'

'To James, I mean?'

'No. I didn't speak to him at all.'

'Did you say anything to Steve?'

'Jesus, Mum — no! Not a word. To anybody. So you don't have to worry.'

'Good girl. The less said.'

Call Me Al

Al exhaled loudly as he got into the car. It was his fourth day at secondary school.

'How was it? Any better than yesterday?'

'Oh. It was just marvellous. My Geography teacher, Mr Turnbull — it will *always* be a ridiculous name, by the way, Turnbull — well, he's still an absolute delight. Today I learned that he's particularly adept at delivering copies back to students by frisbeeing them AT THEIR FACES. But aside from that and his INCESSANT SMART COMMENTS, he's a charming fellow. Can't wait to see him again tomorrow.'

'I'm not sure that frisbeeing is a word.'

'It is now. Honestly, Mum. Each hour in that place is like a mountain to be scaled.'

'Anything positive happen at all?'

'I can't remember the Maths teacher's name but she wears the same perfume as Granny. You know, the musky one.'

'Well, that's something, I suppose. Familiarity can be comforting.'

'It was familiar, but I don't remember feeling particularly comforted by it.'

I laughed.

'Well, it's certainly better than the smell in here since you got in. What *is* that? Is there something in your bag? Something off — maybe fishy?'

Al's face brightened and suddenly he was hooting with laughter, and the stress of four days dissolved for a moment.

'I totally forgot! I must've got used to it.' He started to lift the left sleeve of his jumper away from his skin, folding it slowly and carefully back onto itself. As he did, little bits of mashed cracker and lumps of some other pasty foodstuff fell onto his lap and the seat. A muffled, rancid smell was unleashed into the car.

'What the hell is that? It stinks. Christ!' I put my hand over my nose and pressed down with my elbow on the four window buttons to open them. 'Is it tuna?'

Al was laughing and retching at once, wagging his arm out his window to release sticky bits.

'And *what* is it doing up your sleeve?'

'It's actually liver pâté. And it's been warming itself up my arm for the last hour.'

'What? Is this some weird boys' school initiation thing?'

He laughed and shook his head.

'I am totally repulsed by you at the moment.'

'You won't believe this, Mum. I didn't get to finish my lunch today because I was trying to find the room where we had bloody choir so I was absolutely starving at the end of double Science. Anyway, I made the mistake of saying so to Callum Mitchell, a cool guy in my class. Well, I don't really know if he's that cool or not, but he seems alright. Anyway, Mitchell said, 'You're in luck,' sets his bag down and takes out a sealed lunchbox, saying, 'I packed more than I needed.'

'I asked him what it was while he was taking the lid off. I sensed disaster, Mum, I really did. 'Chicken liver pâté. On wheaten crackers,' he said. I swear, I nearly gagged on his words.'

I laughed. If there's anything Al hates more than a dry wheaten cracker ('hairy whole-foods'), it's pâté. Any sort of pâté. So he told me how he didn't want to offend this Callum kid because he went to such trouble arranging the pâté on the cracker for him and because he could do with a friend and how, because of blind and dumb panic and idiocy, he couldn't get the words, 'No, I don't eat pâté, but thanks a lot' out.

So instead he pecked at the cracker — 'exhaling through my nose as much as I could' — while Callum looked on. And then he turned his back as though looking up at the clock and crushed the loaded disc, bent his elbow up and stuffed the lot up his sleeve. He turned back to his new friend, mock-chewing.

'Did you plump your cheeks out?'

'Oh, yes. I think I might have even rubbed my stomach, you know. To show just how delicious it was. It was a very subtle performance. God Almighty — I actually do stink.'

'Well, I hope you and Callum bonded because the smell's likely to have put off any other potential friends.'

When we pulled in to the driveway, he opened the car door and took the jumper off. With it inside out, we winced at the balled-up bits of pâté stuck to the wool in the crease of the elbow.

'I forgot that I had liver smeared up my arm. *That's* how much I hate that school.'

And then we saw Mae, smiling at us and banging on the sitting room window with her little fists. As we got to the front door, we heard her footsteps and her voice through it. 'Al! Home. Al. Home!' Squeals of delight tumbled out of the house once my keys turned the lock.

She wrapped her arms around her brother's legs and put her cheek against them.

Then she turned to me and pointed. 'Al! Home.'

'Yes, darling, he is. Al is home from school. Isn't it great?'

Al bent down to her, their faces close enough that the tips of their noses were touching. Mae looked into his eyes.

'Smil-ing,' she sang, but there was a worry in her voice. It was a question. Al heard it.

'Yes, Al is smiling,' he said and mirrored her beaming expression back at her.

'Luvoo.'

'I love you too, Mae. You're a legend,' and he put his arms around her and held her tight.

'SMELL!' and she pinched her fingers over her scrunched-up nose.

'It's a funny story actually, Mae,' he said as the three of us walked down the hall. 'Where's Dad? I'll tell you both together.'

★ ★ ★

'Do they . . . do they kill babies like Mae, you know, ones with Down's, in China?' It was later that evening and my son had his back to me.

'Good Lord! I don't think so. That's monstrous.' I tried to keep my voice even. 'Where did you hear that?'

126

'Some asshole in school said it.' His voice was wobbly.

'Well, he's monstrous too.'

'It's crazy, isn't it?'

'Not the pâté guy?'

'No, no. He's OK. It was some other kid that I don't really know. I don't even think he knows about Mae. He might have been just talking, you know.'

I put down the socks I was pairing and sat on his bed.

'I've been thinking about her all day since he said it.' He stopped for a moment. 'You know the way she reaches her arm up and checks the bolt is on the front door before she goes to bed at night? As if she's taking care of all of us? That's really cool.'

Al kept his eyes down while he was talking, his fingers playing with his shoelace.

'And she's clever too. The way she lies all her clothes for the next day out flat, you know? So it's like a little person lying on the floor. That's great.'

I smiled.

'Seriously, when I look in on her before I get into bed and see them arranged, her little tights like skinny legs stopping at the tops of her shoes — it cracks me up, every time.'

I joined in. 'And when she squints and tilts her head back when we go swimming to keep her goggles from sliding down her face. Because she can't get the strap just tight enough to keep them up but she doesn't want anybody's help. I always think that's cute.'

He let the shoelace go and looked at me.

'Mae'll be OK, Mum. Won't she?'

'Of course she will.'

'Because she definitely learns things. You remember when we all thought she'd never manage that twenty-piece jigsaw Grandad bought her. But she did. Because we showed her the secret to it: you just have to do the hard edges first. And she did. She found all the edges and arranged them.'

'You're completely right, Al. Mae is great and that guy is an asshole.'

⋆   ⋆   ⋆

'Where's Alex?'

That Saturday evening my mother was sitting at our kitchen table having tea. Mae was next to her, eating a giant chocolate chip cookie right down the middle so she was up to her ears in it on both sides. She had the look of a very focused duck-billed platypus.

'He's out painting with his friend Issa. You've met Sommer — Issa's mother — well, she cleared a space for their canvases and boards in his back garden so they can use

128

their paints and sprays there to work on their projects without bothering anyone.'

'*Summer* and *Issa?* Are they that coloured family?'

'Sommer. With an 'o'. And, yes, Mum, they're black. As well you know.'

'I see. Anyway, he seems very keen on *art*.'

'He loves it. And he's really quite good. I'm delighted he's found something he enjoys at his new school.'

'And you don't mind?'

'Mind what?'

'Well, of course you wouldn't mind. You had a tendency toward art yourself at that age. Out the door we were with folders of art projects and paintings. I'll never forget it.'

'It was the best part of my week.'

'But it was just so time-consuming. And all the papers and the mess. It took up so much space in the house, which didn't suit me at all, Beth. And I mean, as a subject, it doesn't do anyone any good. Not really. Does it? And if it wasn't art you were at, it was bits of poetry and writing stories. They were the only things you ever showed any interest in.' She shook her head at the memory and nibbled on a cupcake. 'Art's hardly going to make a doctor or a lawyer of him, is it? Hopefully you'll be able to get him out of it once he settles a bit at school.'

'I've no intention of discouraging it.'

'Don't get me wrong — I'm sure it can be marvellous. As a hobby. Ellie Morris swears by it for keeping her stress levels down. She paints pineapples and other difficult fruits. And they're very nice, despite what anyone may think of Ellie. Myself included. But it's not really a 'subject', darling, is it? Trust me — you'll need to nip this in the bud soon enough. It took me months to talk you round before you would give it up.'

'What?'

'Remember? You must've been fourteen or fifteen.'

'I do remember. You told me the teacher said I'd be lucky to scrape a pass in it. I was devastated.'

'I did what any mother of an academic child would do. Of course, there wasn't much I could do to dissuade you from writing. But that seemed to go alright for you in the end, workwise. Well, for a while anyway.' She stood up and opened my fridge door. 'Are you due to do the shopping? There's precious little in here.'

Al walked into the kitchen.

'Hello Alex, darling. I'm glad you're home. I don't like to think of you out wandering the streets in the evening.' I watched my mother air-kiss her grandson.

'Hi Granny. I didn't realise you were calling in.' Al was taking off his army-look jacket as he spoke. 'Mum, two guys in a souped-up car just drove by and shouted 'faggot' — sorry, Granny, but they said it, not me — at me. Do you think it's because of these trousers?' He raised his leg nearer my eye level that I might get a better view.

'No, I don't. I think it's because they're morons,' I said, swerving around his leg.

'Honestly. Are these the kind of conversations you have now? I'm glad I'm not asked here more often.'

I turned to Al. 'Hang up your jacket and you can join us for tea.'

'Coolio.'

He kissed Mae on the forehead and moved her juice cup in from the edge of the table and the path of her elbow as he left the room.

'I certainly don't think it's necessary that he *dresses* like an 'artist' when he's out with his foreign friend,' my mother said loudly before he was out of earshot.

'Actually, Mum, I'm OK,' Al called back. 'I think I'll just go into the sitting room and listen to my music.' And with two enormous fluorescent green headphones, my son simply blocked my mother out.

The Test

Steve and I were in separate cars driving in the dark.

I was following him down the confines of a tortuous country road to his colleague Amanda's house for a dinner party. He was coming straight from the Dublin office so I'd met him in town in my own car. We'd been to this house twice before but he'd always driven us; now, with rain hitting the windscreen like stones being chucked from a bucket, the route was completely unknown to me.

The noisy, wet darkness, the sudden bends, and the brambles scraping into the door made it difficult to keep Steve in sight. I turned off the radio to concentrate on the blurred rectangles of his back lights. I was warm and prickly but kept the fan heater up full to clear the window. I wanted to phone him to tell him to slow down, to hear his voice, but my mobile was in my bag on the floor behind my seat. The road was barely wide enough for one-way traffic and the overhang of tall trees reached across both sides of it creating a sinister canopy.

And then his lights vanished and the

darkness was absolute.

I drove on, uneasy. There was nowhere to pull in and I knew I'd eventually come to a house, hopefully the one I was expected at. And Steve would surely notice me no longer right behind him and do something.

Almost ten minutes and a number of bad bends and guessed turns later, I knew I was lost. I stopped where I was, turned my hazard lights on and leaned my elbow on the central locking button. Reaching for my bag, I prayed for mobile coverage. I found my phone and called Steve.

'Where are you?' he answered immediately. Inoffensive jazzy music was meandering in the background.

'I don't know. I'm lost.'

'You're lost?' I heard a smile in his voice which made him feel further from me. 'But we were only a couple of minutes away and you were still behind me.'

'I know. But it was hard to keep up and then something happened and I couldn't see your lights anymore.'

'I turned them off.'

'What?'

'I turned my lights off to see if you could find your way. Just the last little bit.'

'What?'

'We were practically here.'

'Why would you do that?' A low-hanging branch slapped the roof of the car.

'Just to see, you know. If you could get here. I thought you'd find your way yourself. We've been here before.'

My eyes filled with tears and I felt ridiculous.

'Beth? Can you hear me? Are you still there?'

'Yes.'

'Where exactly are you?'

'I don't fucking know where I am. There are horrible big trees and nothing else.'

'Listen, just stay on the phone. I'll come out and find you.'

'I can't believe you turned your lights off.'

'I thought you'd get here, you know. Delighted with yourself. Or else, you'd call me. Like you have.'

Behind him, I heard Amanda's voice. 'Is that Beth? Where is she?'

'She's just got a bit lost' to her.

'Oh, the poor thing. On such a horrible night. I thought she was following you?' to him.

'It's OK. I'm going to go out and get her' to her.

'Aren't you the perfect husband!' to him.

'I'm coming for you now. Just stay where you are,' he said down the phone.

'What the fuck?' My words were slow and deliberate.

Steve was bent over at my driver's window trying to get his head inside for shelter, his car parked up by the ditch ahead.

'I knew you'd be mad.'

'*What?* Of course I'm mad!' I spoke loudly, despite our heads being only inches apart. 'Anyone would be mad. What were you thinking?'

'I just wanted to see how you'd get on, on your own. For you to see — '

'This horrible, shitty night and you turn your lights off on purpose. *You knew* I would never find my way. *You knew* I wouldn't be able to.'

'I knew you'd call if you needed me, and you did, so — '

'Oh my God. Was this some kind of weird big-man helpless-woman thing?'

He moved his face back and his words got grabbed by the wind as he said them — 'I just thought you might see that I'm — '

'You *wanted* me to be lost, to feel scared so that I would call you for help? So that you could come and save me?'

'No. Well, something like that, maybe. So what?'

'I cannot believe this.'

'Is it so wrong for me to want you to need me, ever? For my wife to even fucking value me at all?'

'Seriously, Steve? You scared me so you could feel like you were rescuing me?'

'No, not for me. For *you*.' His face came back in beside mine, our noses barely apart. 'So *you* could feel like I was rescuing you. So *you* might think that I was good for something. So *you* might see something attractive in me.' Then quieter — 'It sounds fucking stupid out loud.'

'That's because it *is* stupid, Steve. You know, I actually think you're completely crazy.'

'Well, maybe I am. But you know, I wasn't always, Beth. I wasn't always. And you weren't always so — so serious.'

'*So serious?* I wasn't always so serious because my life wasn't so serious. And I wasn't lost in the middle of nowhere. In the fucking rain. Trying to get to some place I don't even want to go. My life wasn't always nothing but a series of obligations and facilitating *everyone else's* lives and what *they need*, and *being nothing*, every day, all the time.'

Cracks were spreading out from our very foundation, like an earthquake gathering

136

ground beneath us.

'Oh come on, Beth. You can be whatever you want.'

'No, I fucking can't, Steve. NO I CAN'T. *You* can. You can turn off your lights and you can go to a party and you can live your life and set yourself new goals. And be important at work. Always *at work,* wherever the fuck that is. But anything I do, EVERYTHING, is purely — *decorative.* That's all. Everything is a stupid triviality when set beside having a profoundly disabled child. So why bother? Why should I fucking bother fooling myself with a distraction or a part-time job, because that's all it would be. A distraction.'

'Listen, Beth, I'm sorry things haven't fucking worked out how you would have hoped. But you have choices and you can make changes, if that's what you *think* you want. If that would stop you being so miserable all the time, I'm ALL fucking for it.'

'You have no idea, Steve. NO IDEA. You travel and get promoted, nothing holding you back. I will always be the parent, *the mother* of a child who won't ever grow up. I *used* to be other things. I *used* to have a career, be a colleague, a woman who had one wardrobe full of clothes *for work* and one for *going out.* But now I *can't* be whatever I want. I can't move forward, I can't move at all, and I can't even go backwards to what my old life was. I have to accept that. I *am* accepting that. But I don't have to put up with your — '

Steve snorted and took a step back from my car.

'You don't accept it at all.' His voice was raised. 'I'm sorry everything is such a disappointment for you. But this is it. Us.' He motioned to himself. 'This is me.'

'Well, aren't I lucky?' I snarled. 'I'm going home, Steve. Back to where I can be responsible and serious and bored. But at least I'll know where I am. And I can find my way back there by myself so I don't need you now. I actually don't think I need you for anything anymore.'

'You don't hear your words, do you?' he said. 'How they slam down, how they make the person you're throwing them at feel. Seriously, Beth. Where have you gone?'

I turned the key and rolled up my window. After a seven-point turn in the narrow darkness, I headed back toward the desperate lure of familiarity.

Steve followed behind me, separate cars driving in the dark.

A Different Kind of Green

'Who owned the hairbrush?'

'What?' Steve's back was to me so I could only see his loud striped shirt but I could imagine the usual knitted annoyance on his face. 'What hairbrush?'

'There was a cerise pink hairbrush on the side table behind you when you Skyped us from your hotel room yesterday morning.'

He turned around slowly and the moment teetered for a second. The whole bedroom paused, waiting for words that might change everything in it.

He looked stricken so there was no uncertainty in my mind. The floor seemed to tilt then with the weight of the pain on my side of it.

He gave a short cough, the way he did when he felt uneasy. Then, looking at the floor, he sat down on the edge of the bed, his palms flat together between his knees.

'It was . . . I'm so sorry. It was . . . an accident.'

'WHAT was?'

'It didn't mean anything. It was just that one time.' His face was white.

'WHAT WAS?' Panic in my voice. 'What

are you saying?' I pressed the heels of my hands hard into my eye sockets, blinding and glaring my vision.

'You and I haven't been having sex. We've barely been talking. It's been months — '

'So it's MY fault? You screwed someone else but I'm to blame? Is that it? Is that what you're saying? SAY — IT.'

He stood suddenly and grabbed both my hands in his.

'NO! Of course not.'

'You asshole.'

'Please, Beth. I'm sorry. It's the worst thing I've ever done.'

He put his head onto my shoulder and sobbed loudly into my hair, each breath and cry being torn out of him. I could feel his tears against my neck and I hated him. Hated that he thought I should comfort him now.

'What have you done? To us. To our life.' I pushed him away.

'It was just one time.'

'With who? Who was it?'

'Nobody.'

'Did you not think about me? About Mae and Al?'

'I never stop thinking about you. Never.'

'Well, you can stop now. Because it's all gone. It's over. We're over, so I hope she was worth it.'

'No, Beth. Don't say that. Please. I don't want us to end. I wasn't looking for someone else. I don't want to be without you.'

'Clearly you can do very fucking well for yourself without me.'

'I can't. You, and the kids. You're everything. Please. I'm so sorry. I was flattered. That someone would want me. Stupid, I know.'

'WHO WAS SHE?'

I watched him thinking about her, about this woman, about sex with her, and I felt a sick rage. 'You gave up your family for what? FOR WHO?'

'Nobody. A stranger. Nothing.'

'I WANT TO KNOW. Do I know her?'

'No! I don't even know her. I met her in the bar at the hotel. She was just there, sitting next to me.'

'A hotel bar?' I snorted. 'Are you joking? My God. It's like a terrible movie.'

'Beth, we don't need to go through this. She was nothing.'

While he spoke, I was imagining him kissing her, slowly first and then more urgently. In my head, she was gorgeous, young. My heart was thunderous in my ears.

'I'm so, so sorry.'

Hot tears were running down my face and my breaths came in gulps and judders.

'Beth, honey. Please. You are my whole life. It was wrong. Stupid of me.' He was standing, his brown eyes full, his arms out to hold me.

I could see him gathering her into the strength of those arms, that body. Those dark eyes taking her in.

'I need to hear it all,' I said, rubbing my hand over my face, a slimy hot mess. 'Is she from work? Is she pretty?'

'No.'

' 'No' to what?' I didn't wait for an answer. 'Did you invite her for drinks back in your room?'

'Please stop, Beth.'

'Why did she bring her hairbrush with her? To your hotel room. Was she planning on staying a while? Did you MESS UP HER FUCKING HAIR?'

'Beth, please. We don't need to do this.'

'YES, WE DO,' I shouted. 'I need to know what you did. What you said. Does she think you're single or just unhappily married? Tell me. I'm serious, Steve. Tell me now.'

I needed to see the cliff so I could decide whether to hold on to the edge or jump off.

So he told me. Like an addict in recovery he recalled the evening aloud, reliving how they'd had a few drinks in the bar at the airport hotel and talked about their work,

142

their lives. They'd gone back to his room and she'd left early the following morning. He hadn't taken her number or given her his. He only knew her first name — Jane.

When he was finished, he sat quietly on the edge of the bed with his eyes closed. He looked like a tired child.

'Please, Beth, I'm begging you. It's the worst thing I've ever done in my life.'

'And just after she left, you opened up your laptop and called me and the kids.' I lay in a ball on the bed.

We stayed there in the silence, our backs to each other, on opposite sides, for a long time.

*   *   *

The light in the room had become dusky when he interrupted the quiet and spoke.

'I remember the day after Mae was born. I remember seeing you, your head bent over her, your face broken. You'd always been so strong, Beth. You were always certain of things, and it made me confident. But that day, that day you were lost in a way that terrified me. I think I panic, you know, I think I feel I'm lost when you are.'

'Steve — don't. Please don't use our daughter as an excuse for you having sex with a stranger.'

'I'm not. Really I'm not. But I do want to talk to you. That's what went wrong — we shut down to each other.' He waited for me to respond but I stayed silent, stayed shut down. So he continued.

'I hated that old hospital with its long polished corridors and its iron beds. I hated being so helpless, hated that nobody had anything to offer, that nobody was in control. I wanted you to have the answers, to reassure me. How selfish is that?' He laughed a little, hearing his words. 'I've never wanted to go home so much as on that day. The peeling blue walls, the rattling windows and the wails of women: I wanted to run from all of it. The wintry sky outside was so dark and the red-bricked buildings so cold-looking, so neglected. I wanted to gather you and Mae up out of the place and get Al and just go, just take the three of you home to New Zealand, so things could be brighter, greener.' His voice was quiet and full of melancholy. 'People talk about how green Ireland is but I don't really see it. It's often a kind of grey to me, or maybe — maybe it is green. Just a different kind of green.'

He stood up and went to the window and rested his forehead on it.

And I hated him, everything about him, the back of his head, the curve of his shoulders.

Or maybe it was love.

After a moment he spoke — 'Bloody Anna is waving up from across the street. She misses nothing, that one. Nothing. I've never liked her. Do you know that when Mae was just a newborn, sleeping in her basket in the kitchen, Anna tutted about her snoring. Mae lying there like a delicate bird — do you remember, the way she looked when she was so tiny? Anyway, she was doing her soft, whistling snore. I said something silly about it being a long-standing O'Connor trait, I don't remember exactly. But Anna just said she was 'a funny little thing' which I thought was weird. *And then* she said she wondered if Mae was snoring *'because of her condition'*. For fuck's sake. It drives me mad, Beth. Things around here are driving me mad.'

He turned from the window to look at me. 'But I love you. I absolutely do. And I never ever meant to hurt you. I'm begging you. Please believe me.'

He came and knelt at the side of the bed where I lay and put his hand lightly on mine. 'Tell me what to do. Anything. Please.' His face was anguished and his voice ached, his gentle words at odds with the loud shirt he was wearing.

I closed my eyes. He took his hand away but still stayed on his knees.

'Please, Beth.'

'I need you to leave. You can't stay here.'

'Where will I go?' His hands were raised in front of him, searching. 'I don't know how to go. Where to go. Can we even afford for me to leave?'

'I won't be organising it for you, Steve. Just leave. Figure things out for yourself, for once.'

'I'm begging, Beth — please don't give up on me. Let me stay and make this better.'

'You have to go.'

'I'll move in to the spare room.'

'I need you to leave this house now — before the kids get home.' My voice was tired and old.

'OK, if it's what you want then — '

As he stood and moved away, the wooden floor creaked beneath his feet as it always did. But today the creaking was unbearable.

I heard him pulling down the case he had used for his trip earlier this week, the one I had packed for him. I opened my eyes and watched him choosing what to bring.

'You should bring enough for a while.'

I saw the back of his head nod. He grabbed shirts and trousers and dumped them into the case, ironing the top layer of the crumpled pile with the flat of his hands. No underwear, no shoes. But it wasn't for me to tell him anymore.

He zipped up the case and turned to me.

'I will spend the rest of my life making this right, if you will let me. Please let me. Please try to forgive me. Tell Al and Mae I'm just gone away for a few days for work,' he cried as he forced the words out, 'and that I love them both so very much.'

He picked up his jacket and held it in a ball against his chest, a heartbroken teenager. I turned away and he left the room.

*   *   *

That night in our bed, I remembered a woman in the local grocery shop telling me about her cousin who'd had a baby with Down syndrome.

'He's fifteen now and not a bother on him — goes to normal school and seems to take part in most things,' she'd said. 'The marriage went to pieces, though. Fell apart after a year or two. He couldn't handle it — the dad. Never got his head around it.'

Stack upon stack of disappointment and sadness had piled up like dirty laundry between Steve and me for so long that it had become easier to do things separately than together. Two employees working separate shifts in a non-profit, tedious business.

I saw that I could get out now. That I was

already out, in a way. He'd handed me a golden ticket. Nobody could blame me for leaving now. The opportunity to collapse my marriage both thrilled and terrified me. I wouldn't have to listen to the fork scraping off his teeth when he was eating, or watch him swishing his tea around the sides of his cup before taking a gulp, or hear him scratching the sole of one foot with the nails from the other.

I pictured myself in a small apartment by the sea with Al and Mae, away from the linen trousers and the kitchen islands. I would be a middle-aged, single mother who didn't have sex only half of the time. With the other half of my time — when Steve took our children — I could do any number of stupid things and pretend to be free. I could leave hairbrushes in strangers' hotel rooms.

But then I imagined him running his hand up this woman's thigh while our daughter drew a picture for him, here, in her pyjamas. And I cried painfully, the sounds wrenching from the deepest part of me. On the side of the bed that had been Steve's for so many years, Mae coughed wetly, her lungs dampened by weather which attacked her extra chromosome in her sleep.

The Hard Edges

My son was distraught.

His first romance had begun and ended in the space of three weeks. I looked sideways at his face and felt the weight of his anxious expression.

It was the same expression I'd seen when, as a six-year-old, he sat staring at a plate of teddy-bear-shaped breaded chicken pieces unable to eat them because they were teddies. He was OK with them being chicken.

When, as a seven-year-old, he threatened to 'eat a marker' if Steve and I didn't make up over some silly disagreement.

When, as a ten-year-old, he had to take a certain amount of steps from the bathroom to his bedroom door every night or the house would burn to the ground.

Now, as a fourteen-year-old, he was heartbroken about a girl, and my love for him still pulled on everything around it just as it had when he was an infant.

He took a gulp from his energy drink and started to tinker with the ring pull. I got a bag of Maltesers down from the press and opened them, something to do while he gathered his words for the next instalment of the story.

'So I saw her sitting on the ground with some boys I half-recognised. They're older than me. I don't know how she knows them but I guess they must do cool stuff that I don't or whatever because now she doesn't want to know me anymore.'

How excited and expectant he had been heading out to this disco earlier, choosing his outfit carefully, testing the scents of the antiperspirants left behind on Steve's side of the bathroom. All talk about Lucy.

'She made it clear,' now he took a deep breath, 'that she wasn't interested in talking to me ever again. Even though only two days ago I was 'amazing'. So I stood there on the edge of the dance floor, with these assholes in their skinny jeans looking up at me, smirking and making smart comments, with their long legs taking up all the space, while she sat in the middle of them looking like a stupid, smug kid. I hate her.'

His body loosened and he started to cry, really horribly — all strings of spit and big fat tears and hot, red cheeks. His lips were pulpy and his voice uneven when he eventually got more words out.

'I had to act like I wasn't bothered and pretend I knew other people in the crowd. I was looking for someone familiar but there wasn't anyone. Only her on the floor, laughing at me.' He wiped his nose on the back of his sleeve and caught his breath. 'Life totally sucks, Mum.'

'Sometimes it really does, honey.' I put my arms around him, afraid as I did it that he mightn't want that anymore — that the rules had changed now he was a disco-going teenager who had his first girlfriend behind him. But he hugged me back so I held on.

'When does it get easy?'

'Oh, Al, I don't think it ever gets easy really. We just do our best to figure out which are the hard edges.'

Eoin

I hadn't wanted to go to the party at all. And especially not on my own. The fortieth birthday of an old neighbour whose parents were in the golf club. I promised my mother I would pop in with a gift.

And there was Eoin. I felt my breath catch. I'd often wondered if I'd ever see him again. He leant against the kitchen bar, part of a group, but his familiar voice was the only one travelling. I could see him from the torso up. He had lost none of his apparent self-assurance, all arms and exaggerated expressions. Our eyes met and he started to smile slowly, and then his face lit like a beam. He made his way toward me in that purposeful manner he'd always had: *I am important and everywhere I go is terribly important.*

'Beth O'Connor.' He blew his cheeks out and looked me up and down. 'You beautiful thing.'

The gesture was strangely flattering now I was a forty-three-year-old mother of two whose husband was staying in a shitty apartment because he'd shagged some woman in an airport hotel.

'Eoin Leonard, you charmer.'

'Almost twenty years. That's how long it's been.'

I smiled. 'You never used to know what I was thinking.'

'We were two wonderful people who happened to fall in love and happened to have a pigmentation problem.'

I got it and I laughed. It's from *Guess Who's Coming to Dinner*, a film we watched over and over from beneath a duvet in his flat many years before. He laughs too and already things are familiar.

'And it never occurred to me that I would fall in love with a Negro,' I drawled, 'but I have.'

'There you are. Still my little Katie Hepburn. I've actually been avoiding you for years, you know.'

'Very successfully too.'

'I didn't want to have to think about you more than I already was. Which, it may surprise you to learn, was quite a lot.'

I laughed. 'No, you did not.'

'But here you are. Looking gorgeous. And all on your own, as I see it.'

'God, you really haven't changed. Apart from the obvious weight.'

'Ouch. Are you saying you never thought of me?'

'Never.'

'Harsh, but I'll let it go because I know it's a lie. How's life treating you up on Vesey Hill? You didn't exactly go far from the nest. Vesey Hill.' He half-whistled in admiration. 'I knew you'd do well.'

Embarrassed by my address and shocked that he knew where I lived, I said nothing.

'Well, I haven't a thing to show for my time in this world,' he declared to the room. 'I didn't marry, have no children. But there have been some ladies, I won't lie to you.' He smirked.

'Girls with high approval ratings and a good pedigree, no doubt.'

'Mostly.'

'And they bored you?'

He laughed. 'That they did. It turns out I let the right girl get away. Years ago. A feisty little thing she was.'

Eoin. The one who made me think fast, who made me want to be prettier, wittier, better. *EO-IN EO-IN EO-IN* — I sing it in my head, as though it's a siren. 'He should come with a warning,' Jilly had said.

'Have dinner with me. Please. This weekend. Any night. You choose.'

'What? No! I don't want to. And anyway, as you are probably well aware, I'm married.' *I think.*

'I heard. To some foreign shyster.'

154

I laughed. 'I really should go, Eoin. I just called in to leave a gift.'

'One dinner? With an old friend? Please.'

'Christ. Are you actually begging?'

'I will if I must.'

'You big eejit.'

'I'll even bring you to that low-rent Italian restaurant you always loved. I think it's still there.'

Il Primo. It had red-and-white chequerboard tablecloths and off-white candles stuck in waxed-over Chianti bottles. It unlocked its wooden doors at noon every day and didn't close them again until late into the night. The kind of restaurant beloved of students and readers and talkers. Somewhere I used to go to read and write stories, before life became pointless glossy magazines and over-priced pastries in suburban cafés.

'Maybe.'

'Good enough for me. Here's my card. Call me with a date that suits you.'

'Just two old friends. Catching up,' I said, running my fingers over the raised letters of his name.

'Absolutely.' He wiggled his eyebrows up and down comically. 'Unless you find yourself wanting more.'

'I won't. Bye, Eoin.'

'See you soon, my Katie.' He gave me a

look that cut out everyone else in the room.

I knew his eyes were on me as I left so I did my best walk and, as I did, I realised it'd been a very long time since I'd made that kind of effort.

'Au reservoir,' he called after me. I laughed and felt about fourteen.

⋆   ⋆   ⋆

I'd met him at work.

I was twenty-three and had just started as a copywriter in a web design company. He sat next to me in an open-plan office. I wasn't sure what he did exactly, only that he worked with numbers, but even so, he piqued my interest. He laughed easily. I liked that. It made people feel that they were funny. He made me feel that I was hilarious.

⋆   ⋆   ⋆

He lived alone in a flat on the second floor of a Georgian house, just outside the city centre.

'Your laugh lights this room,' he'd said.

'Just as well, with those curtains always pulled. My laugh provides your vitamin D. Without me in here, you'd have rickets.'

And with that, he'd pulled back the curtains. Every curtain in the flat. Yanked back as far as they would go in an effort at a grand gesture. So much glass always covered. The rooms were lit with the glow from the street lamps.

'Come on.' He'd taken my hand in his and pulled me off the bed. A man leading his woman. We stood in full view at the window. Hand in hand. Me wearing just his T-shirt; he in boxers.

It was 1.30 a.m. so there was nobody to see us.

Cars had passed periodically, making lines on the walls and ceiling.

He'd parked in a car park not too far from Paradiso, where he had booked a table for us. The evening was dark and the rain starting as we walked quickly to its brass-and-glass doors, heads down to avoid wet faces.

We'd stepped into the warmth of the lavish foyer. I'd felt his previously supportive arm tighten on the outside of my shoulder and noticed I was being turned around.

Suddenly, we were leaving the warmth, walking back through the brassy doors, again passing the pair of lollipop topiaries and stepping into the rain.

'There was someone in there . . . '

He kept walking, faster now. Looking over his shoulder. As though he had shoplifted something.

I waited for more words. Trying to keep pace. None came. That was to be it.

I wasn't keeping up. I tensed as I heard myself ask, 'A woman?'

'No, no. A friend. A male friend. Friends actually. Three of them, from the rugby club.'

I relaxed and started to smile.

'I don't mind. I'm sure we can sit over the other side. Avoid them.'

'No. I mind. I don't want to see them at all.'

I sped up. I had to, to be heard.

'I don't understand. They can't be good friends if you'd give up a Saturday-night table in Paradiso not to see them.'

'They're actually really good guys. Although I don't see why that's relevant.' His voice was getting tetchy. I was in the dark and being left there.

We settled into a hurried pace. An unpleasant silence was creeping over us like a damp and cold blanket.

'They think I'm single.'

My stomach lurched. I stopped dead.

'They *think* you are? I also *think* you are. You're not . . . *married?*'

The last word was a whisper.

'No! God, no! No — they think I'm single, sorry, as in Not Seeing Anyone,' looking away now.

He had stopped too and was standing opposite me, but at arm's length. Humouring me with his stillness. I could practically hear his feet itching to move.

It only took a second for the reality of what had just happened to collapse onto me. And when it did, I longed for those moments before enlightenment, to be back when I was just confused.

He had given up a table in Paradiso to avoid being seen with me.

We stood in the rain.

'Am I a secret?'

I thought of how everyone in my circle knew about him, about tonight.

'Well, no. Not a . . . actually, yes. Yes, you kind of are.'

I went on, ignoring the confirmation that I hadn't needed. 'It's like you've been 'caught' with me. Why should you not be with me?' My voice was raised now, not caring who might hear or turn to see.

He picked up the pace once more. I was running alongside in my red ballet pumps. His face was impatient; I was a spoiled child angry about not being bought a pony. About not having it all.

He was almost marching now. I kept veering in — You Cannot Get Away — he kept veering out. Two people, holding each other close, would have comfortably walked between us. His right side was almost skimming the shopfronts at the path's edge.

'Why am I a secret? Why?' I could hear my tone hardening. Directed at the side of his face.

'I'm just not ready for all that. I'd rather be . . . discreet.'

He dived into the garish light of the car park's pay station.

'Let's go back to my place,' his attempt at chirpiness, like the bottom hadn't just fallen out of our farce.

I stayed silent.

He put the ticket in the machine — £2.00 appeared on the screen. I'd never known parking so cheap in the city centre, but then I'd never known such a swift stay. So that was what returning within the first sixty minutes looked like: £2.00.

He put a crisp £50 note into the slot. He hadn't come prepared for fleeing the scene.

Clank-Clank-Clank-Clank-Clank-Clank-Clank.

Twenty-four times.

The sound of every coin that fell as change had amplified in the hollow between us.

I'd loved the nights and the earliest part of the mornings.

But then car doors would open and shut

160

outside, engines would start, voices in the flats and streets around us would become more frequent, the real world encroaching.

I'd watch him arc away from me and feel his half of the intimacy we shared dissolve. He'd leave the room naked and return in a suit, all business.

I'd have dressed quickly and made the bed while he was in the bathroom, tidying the scene.

He'd stand in the doorway, his outside smile in place: 'Let's go then, Katie Koo.'

'Righty-oh.'

I'd say nothing more lest it disturb the delicate pretence. To protect it, so I could keep it.

Occasionally, a wedding invitation would request the pleasure of the company of 'Eoin plus Guest'. I hated these embossed cards, lurking behind the clock in his sitting room. He never asked me to go, and I never asked why not.

Once, I gave him a lift. It was a still and sunny afternoon as he walked up the incline and into the cluck of early birds admiring each other outside the church, clasping envelope purses.

He waved me off, waved me away.

At 12.05 a.m., he'd phoned. I was still up, hoping he would.

But it wasn't a call at all. It was just distant footstep sounds — the noise of a crotch, of mumbled talking, of someone walking, having accidentally phoned you with their pocket, with their legs.

In his bed a week or so later, I noticed a tiny sticker — a perfectly square white box with a red bow at its top. A sticker no bigger than my smallest fingernail stuck in the middle of the headboard. Cute. Stuck there by a girl. It was new, left within the last five days. My stomach sank into my back.

I wanted to meet her and ask her what it was that she saw in him.

He saw me looking at the sticker.

I'd made my mouth do a smile. *Nice gift.*

He'd left me a voice message when the first fortnight in forever passed without my contacting him. He was at a charity blind-date ball.

'I only came because I thought you might be here. And blind enough to date me. Miss you.'

I was at home, It was 1.55 a.m. If he meant it, he'd follow it up at a reasonable hour. In the sobriety of daylight.

He didn't. And it had been years. Nearly twenty of them.

★ ★ ★

An envelope with *Katie* written on the front came through my letterbox two days after our middle-aged reunion. Inside, an expensive-looking card informed me that Eoin Leonard was waiting to take my call. I laughed. I phoned the number he had highlighted in yellow, drawn a heart around and stuck a Post-it with an arrow on it beside.

'I got your card. Very Jane Austen.'

'Good. Think of me as your own Fanny Price.'

'It's a little creepy.'

'The fanny thing?'

'No. To think you were standing in my garden in the middle of the day.'

'I wasn't. My PA was. On her lunch break.'

'I had actually totally forgotten about you. Again.'

'Ha.' He had heard the smile in my voice. 'I've a good mind to come over there and spank your bottom right now for that fib.'

★ ★ ★

Eoin pushed back the creaky door, his hand high enough up for me to pass under. As I followed the waitress to our table, he slipped his arm around my waist like none of my other friends ever did.

'So, you stopped calling me some time

163

back — ' he checked his watch — 'in the nineties. What was that about?' He speared an olive with a cocktail stick, smirking.

'You were acting the maggot. I couldn't wait around while you decided what you wanted. *Who* you wanted. I'd have been waiting forever.'

'Correction. You'd have been waiting until now. I was an idiot, afraid of commitment. Back then.'

The conversation was already in danger of taking a turn into deep and murky waters.

'God, Katie, I was so crazy about you. But I was always afraid you would leave me.' And in he dived, head first, no life jacket. 'When we were together and I kept you a secret, it was because I was afraid you would leave me. That everyone would know us together, and then you would leave me. You were so lovely about us. But you would have left and everyone would've known that I'd failed. I wouldn't be good at managing that.' He put his hand over mine. 'I'm sorry.'

'You were afraid of me?' I laughed.

'I adored you. Probably a bit too much.'

'Ha! I was never enough for you, you shit.'

'You're certainly enough for me now, Katie. Lordy. The size of you,' he said. 'No, honestly, you look beautiful, Beth. A picture.'

164

The waiter was standing over us.

'Can I get you anything more? Desserts? Coffees?'

'She doesn't drink coffee. She never liked it.' Eoin was speaking directly to him. 'Coffee and underground car parks — the two things she can't bear.'

I didn't say that over the last decade or two the list of things I couldn't bear had grown like a weed. Or that my husband had screwed a stranger just over a month ago. Five weeks to the day, actually. Or that I was lonely, so achingly lonely.

'Oh, wow! Beth and Eoin! It *is* you.' A woman was coming toward our table, shrieking. 'I saw you but thought *'It can't be'* but it *is*! I recognise you both because you're together, you know *in context*. It's me. Rosemary Duggan? Well, I'm Byrne now. But you'd remember me as Duggan. We all worked together in that web place back in the heyday. It must be twenty years ago!'

'Rosemary. Of course.' Eoin answered her.

I sat silently, feeling like I'd been caught in the act, although just what the act was I didn't know.

'You both look amazing. I can't believe you guys got together! And are still together!' She put her hand over her heart and tilted her face to the side: 'I think I remember hearing a rumour about you two at the time but you — ' she poked Eoin in the chest with each word — 'but you denied it, as I recall!'

Eoin hunched up his shoulders to get her finger off him and half-laughed while squeezing my hand.

'We're not actually together at all, Rosemary.' I moved my hand away. 'I pretty much haven't seen Eoin since you have.' I showed up my wedding finger. 'Married. To someone else.'

'Well, he must be verrrrry understanding of this little *arrangement*! And I think I'll leave you to it!' She laughed and slapped my hand hard before walking away.

'Christ,' I said, rubbing my hand. 'Now she thinks we're having an affair.'

'The fool.'

★   ★   ★

Another car park with Eoin.

But different this time. Now he didn't care who saw. I did.

'It is so lovely to see you again, Katie.' He rocked back on his heels. And something about the way he did it was so familiar. The suited man after his morning shower.

166

'I've thought about you, about us, so many times.'

'No you haven't!' I laughed, taking a step away from him.

He took two steps forward and his hands came up to my face and he held it. 'I don't think I've ever wanted someone so much.'

I knew my skin was flushed. I didn't lift my face to his. He lowered his head and nudged my nose up with his nose, so our eyes were level.

With his hand pressing on the small of my back, he kissed me.

He pulled me in by the hand and kissed me again. Pressing my mouth harder this time. More determined and, with every moment, more attractive.

'Nobody has ever made me happy like you did. In all of those years. I made a terrible mistake letting you go.'

'We should talk about this *inside* the car.'

He made no effort to move. Now he was all about the public display. 'Give me a chance, Katie.'

'What about my husband?' I was reeling.

'Grrrr. Him again!' he said in his best menacing voice, which made me smile. 'Forget him. I will look after you. Where is he now anyway?'

I ignored the question. 'And my children?'

I asked, eyebrows raised.

'I will be their friend, the best friend I can be.' His voice became gentle, serious. 'Of course, Beth. I need you in my life.'

His hand brushed my upper arm, the side of my breast. I held my breath and stood rigid, waiting for his next move. With his other hand he circled around the curve of my back, before pulling me close so our bodies were against each other. I inclined my face this time. Just for a moment.

Three kisses. Now that's asking for trouble.

'Do you want to come home with me?'

'No.'

The wine — or maybe that last kiss — had unglued me and my head felt undone, like my skull was relaxing, *softening*, and all kinds of overblown words and feelings might just spill from me any second.

'Do you think you could love me again?'

'I doubt it.' *I hope not.*

He held my gaze. 'Well, I'll wait until you don't doubt it.'

★   ★   ★

I relived the evening over and over in my head the next day and my body felt awake, alive.

'There's no part of you that I can't recall,'

he had said. And he'd sat back, squeezed his eyes shut as though pulling a file from a mental cabinet, and smiled.

I thought about my paralysingly adequate life. And how Steve had been unfaithful. How he had done this first. He had started it.

The possibility that I might have options, that a man — that *this* man whom I had once wanted more than anything — would now offer me something, would desire me, at this stage of my life, was thrilling. Completely stupid, but thrilling too.

Leaving the house to collect Mae from her speech therapy session, I reversed into the wheelie bin, which toppled over spilling our refuse onto the path, knocking into Al's free-standing basketball net on its way down, causing it to crash forward into the middle of the street.

It was a moment of chaos in Vesey Hill. And it felt good to have caused it.

★ ★ ★

Eoin smiled and shook his head slowly as he looked at the photograph of my daughter.

'You can see she has Down syndrome?' I asked lightly.

'I can see that she has lovely almond eyes. And that she has her mum's beautiful mouth.

169

And that she's a little dote. I would barely have noticed it.'

A dam burst inside me and relief shot through every part of my body and I had to stop myself from thanking him for saying that.

'Keep Saturday night free,' he said as he stood up. 'And Sunday morning.'

★   ★   ★

The next day, a second envelope for *Katie* landed on the mat behind my letterbox.

My Katie,
I'm afraid of how much I love you. I'm afraid because I don't think you're free to love me recklessly and completely.

I raised my eyes from the letter and looked at my daughter sitting at the kitchen table. She was carefully stretching and unpleating the silver case around a cupcake. When she had separated the entire sponge from its casing, she removed it and balanced the cake on her palm to admire it for a moment. She started to nibble at the edges of the pink frosting.

I looked back down at the page.

I will always care deeply for you. And I feel that in the future, when things are

*simpler and freer, we will find each other
and we will be together.*

*I still really want to take you away for
Saturday night —*

'I'm sure you do.'

*But I want to say upfront that I can't see
a future for us after that, for now. I
couldn't bear you to think that this is
because of your gorgeous daughter and
her diagnosis. And yet we both know I
can just about manage to take care of
myself.*

'You shit.'
Mae looked up, her eyes wide. It wasn't a
word or a tone that she was familiar with. She
read my face and gave a little laugh.
And I started to laugh too. Mae clapped
her little flat hands together.
'Honestly, Mae. If only you knew.' I
laughed at his words, at my own stupidity.
I would barely have noticed it. 'What a
complete shit.'
'SHIT!' said Mae.
Oh God! But she said it so precisely. The
notoriously difficult 'sh' sound. So clearly, no
furry edges.
'Well done, Mae! Yes! That's right — shit

— good girl.' I cupped my hands around her beaming face.

And our laughter picked up again. Our heads tilted back now. Mae clapping. When we managed to stop, I wiped tears from my eyes and we grinned at each other.

Please say you'll come. You and I, Saturday night, no strings. I promise you'll enjoy it.
Love Eoin x

I saw now that I would never solve the puzzle of Eoin because there was no puzzle, no riddle to untangle. He was just a charming, silly, self-serving chancer. And I had been nothing more than a fool.

★　★　★

As I brought her up to bed that evening, Mae pointed to Steve in the photo hanging by the stairs.

'Dada,' she said and, tilting her head to the side, she hugged herself and looked into my eyes.

'Yes. Dada.' I smiled back.

And I saw how simple it was to be foolish and I understood how horrible, ugly mistakes could easily be made.

Teacups and Tepees

Steve was standing, clean-shaven and neatly dressed, outside a shop that fixes broken mobile phones. He was pulling the zip on his jacket up and down, his eyes darting around the street. Then he saw me and almost ran the few yards between us.

'I was afraid you wouldn't come,' he said, with a nervous smile.

'I said I would.'

'I know, but I was afraid you might think I needed to be left. To be left standing.'

His face was pale and penitent-looking. A man in a suit pushed between us, knocking him a little to one side. Steve apologised to him and then to me.

The afternoon itself was pallid and unsure, clouding over and then brightening. In the window of the furrier opposite, an older man rearranged two coats and stood back to consider the change.

Nobody seemed to know what to do with themselves.

I had spent all of yesterday waiting for it to be night, so that this day could be allowed to begin. I wanted to see him. And yet it would be painful, this talking and thinking and aching about raw things as it seemed we must.

It had been only six weeks since I had asked him to leave our home, only one week since Eoin.

'Do you want a crêpe? I know how you like those.' He motioned at the hot plates on wheels that were parked a little further down the street. 'I could get you one with chocolate or whatever. You choose. We could walk with them. Or we could sit down somewhere. Whatever you like.'

A council worker pulled up in a van and started to unload traffic cones next to us.

'You can't stand there, bud. I need this area. You might be better off trying to win her over inside, out of the way.' He laughed and gave me a wink.

I ignored him.

'Let's get a table there,' I said to Steve and pointed at the little Spanish café where the corner met Grafton Street a few shops down.

'OK. Perfect.'

We walked together, a quiet distance between us, our fingertips brushing just once.

We passed the flower stalls in the centre of the street; tall, graceful lilies and fat, bulbous tulips in every colour stood proudly in black plastic buckets. The flower seller was dressed in men's rain gear with an oversized sleeveless jacket and ungainly brown work boots. Her black-dyed hair was pulled back into a ponytail, straggly pieces standing on end around her face like she'd had a fright in a cartoon. She was giving an elegantly dressed woman her change, counting coins into her palm from deeply buried pockets.

We sat at a table outside, under the canopy and next to the heater. I thought there would be more to distract us out there, more to fill the spaces when our words ran scared.

The waitress came back with our teapot and cups. We sat watching her move spoons around and clear away glasses. Then we both thanked her more than was necessary, happy with the opportunity to use our voices and remind each other that we actually were nice, pleasant people.

At tables around us, men and women ate and drank and spoke.

The restaurant Paradiso was on the opposite side of the street. I'd still never eaten there. An anxious-looking woman stood outside it, clinging onto the shoulder strap of her handbag.

'Your wrists are very thin,' Steve said, with concern.

My hands were clasped on the table edge, nun-like.

I lifted them and placed them around my cup for a moment before putting them down onto my lap. I'd mentioned to my mother that I'd lost weight over the last month or so. 'Isn't that marvellous?' she had said. 'Don't get rid of your clothes, though, Beth; you might feel happy again some time.'

She'd cried when I first told her about Steve and me.

'How could he do this to us?' she wept.

'He didn't have to tell you, you know. He could have easily made up something about the hairbrush. He didn't have to admit to anything,' my father had said.

* * *

'Thank you for meeting me, Beth. I love you. More than I can ever say. I'm so sorry for what I've done.'

From the way Steve held his shoulders and the way his eyes stayed on mine while he spoke, I knew that it was true.

The first couple of weeks after he'd left, I'd followed my body around while it did its best with the practical things that had to be done: the school run, the laundry, the habits of the last decade. I prepared meals for three trying not to cry into the pan every time.

Sommer was the best person for a terrible

situation. She'd arrive before I even knew I needed her, to hold me together, to hold me up, to tell me that I didn't look *completely* terrible. And I never felt as though I was delaying her or keeping her from other things, although I must have been. So I made it through the days' allotted hours to bedtime where sleep came in short fits, if at all.

I had told Al and Mae that Steve was gone away for work for a while. Al pressed me to know when he'd be back but I just said that it would take as long as these things take. Mae climbed onto my lap to study my face before hugging me for longer than usual.

'What things?' Al asked.

'Contracts,' I said into Mae's hair.

And then there was Eoin, a breezy cloud that had passed over me briefly, of no real use in my life — certainly not the moon he liked to imagine he was — but leaving a new understanding when he floated on.

'I don't know what to say. Or what I can do. It was so stupid. Please tell me. I'm just — sorry.'

'I believe you,' I said. Because I did.

Big, manly tears fell on the table around his cup, one at a time, his eyes taking polite turns.

We spoke for a moment about the children, our voices respectful and gentle with each other as though there was a dead body within earshot.

Women idled by putting umbrellas up and taking them down, stretching a tester arm out, palm upwards, feeling for drizzle. The sky was darkening, clouding over, and the rising wind caused the heater beside us to sway. The street lamps came on — globes with gold stars on them — even though it was just gone four o'clock.

At the far end of the street St Ann's church looked down in the dismal daylight, its red doors locked, its giant circular window an all-seeing eye. An attractive woman at the next table applied lip balm with her finger before offering her friend some. The friend declined, as they always did. I wondered if either of them looked like his Jane. I tried to imagine her being timid and plain, making him feel he was being kind, but I couldn't. She was gorgeous, I knew it. My shoulders shuddered trying to shake off the thought.

'Are you cold? We could go inside. If you want to.'

I shook my head.

I thought how I'd often felt much older than Steve, felt responsible for him. Since the start. Now, right here, I could put the weight of this life with him, of being his wife, down. I could just go home to Mae and Al. But despite the knotted dull pain in my chest, I knew that our life together wasn't over. I hadn't changed his pillow case on the bed since he'd left. I liked the smell of his hair on it.

Three women huddling in dark coats tried to chat, apprehensively eyeing the clouds. The flower seller started to unroll a further plastic mac to put on over her rain gear. Everything was difficult in uncertain weather.

Then the sky burst and the rain that fell was an attack. It silenced all talk at the tables around us. Everyone stared at it, bouncing off bags and off the pavement. Men and women ran past, eyes squinted, shoulders hunched, newspapers pointlessly draped over their heads, wet through in seconds. Some looked straight up as they ran, trying to calculate how much might fall. Two bicycles chained to a railing that had a Bicycles Will Be Removed sign glistened and shone.

I stood up, so that Steve would.

'Will you drive me home?'

'Yes. I'd love to.'

Running toward his car, I remembered the early days and how attractive he was when he was driving, his confidence behind the wheel, the ease with which he swung his arm across the back of my seat and half-turned to reverse out of a parking space. I was so lost in the memory that it was a moment before I noticed that I'd taken his hand in the rain.

★ ★ ★

For the first while after Steve moved back home, I'd feel warm toward him when we were apart during the day. But then I'd see him, up close, arriving into the hall, shutting the front door behind him, an expectant look on his face, and I'd feel barely able to tolerate his existence. Smiling at me when I spoke, nodding at everything I said, choosing the programmes I liked to watch, not texting while I was talking to him: he was the Most Agreeable Man in the World.

I'd think about him wrapped around someone else and the thought would grow and darken and blacken the rest of the day until I could cleave it from its grip on me by burying it in sleep.

I took part in careful conversations and busied myself at the oven when I saw his hand hovering in the air near my waist looking for permission to land. He was auditioning for his old position, making me the tea I preferred with the leaves and the strainer even though he'd always complained it was 'finicky and badly designed'.

I lay on my side with my back to him in

bed. If I was awake when he came into the darkness of our room, I wouldn't move and I'd keep my breathing shallow and quiet. I'd hear him place his shoes quietly on the floor, the rustle of his trousers, the whispered swear as his belt buckle clanged off the radiator, his bumping around in his socks and shirt for another minute, trying not to make noise.

He would slide under the top sheet causing it to lift up and come loose around me. And then he'd lean over and look at the side of my face, waiting to see if my eyes would open, his invitation. I would keep my features still, not ready to let go of my grievance. After a moment, he'd lie back onto his pillow and I'd know he was staring at the ceiling.

One morning he walked in on me changing my clothes. He'd said, 'Sorry,' and kept his eyes averted, making a show instead of checking the bulb and the fitting in the lamp that had been flickering for months. We both heard the glass shower door in the en suite slide and clang shut then, pulled too hard. I looked in and saw Mae sitting in her clothes in the wet shower tray, her gorgeous face clouded with an anxious little scowl.

The Rush

My mother invited the four of us for Sunday tea. The table was set beautifully for a family of dwarves: tiny, ornate cups usually for display purposes only were obscured by mini-brownies for Al and Mae and, in 'bite-sized' portions, my favourite carrot cake muffins.

'It would be great if you could keep that weight off now,' she said, patting my arm.

She spoke to Steve as though they'd just been introduced and she didn't care for the impression he was making. She handed him the chipped white mug she kept for the gardener's sugary tea.

My father gave him a manly handshake.

'Good to have you back. Loyalty is the thing, you know. And let's say no more about it.' But then he did. 'I don't ask for much from my family, but loyalty. And Beth's mother has always given it.'

My mother straightened her back at this high praise and her chest rose.

In the hallway later, he took me aside. 'Beth, if you want your life with Steve to continue, then you have to forgive him. You don't need a reason or rationale — it's simply what must be done.'

★   ★   ★

The following morning, I couldn't stand any more eggshells. Steve and I were circling each other, wary and hurt. Full of hope, full of dread.

'I want us to stand in a field and scream and shout everything at each other, every-thing we've ever wanted to say and haven't, all of it: the disappointments, the small lies, the pain, the congealed resentments, every-thing.'

I drew a breath.

'All the fucking festering things that got us to the point where we didn't know each other anymore and you could have sex with someone else. The things I've done, the things you've done. Everything that has us here, behaving like idiotic, prudish strangers.'

He jumped up.

'Let's go. Let's do it. Let's go somewhere and do it.' He was grabbing our jackets out of the press. 'Now. Come on. It's a fantastic idea.'

'I don't want a bloody jacket. I want you to help me. Make me understand what hap-pened to us.' I was shouting. 'Make me.'

183

I went to push the jacket, to push him away.

'Beat me and rage at me, Beth, but you will not push me away. I won't let you leave me. I will fight, really, I will fight until you let go and love me again.'

I stood glowering at him.

'I made a mistake, Beth. And I won't ever forgive myself for it. I just felt like I'd been watching myself from the outside moving through a life, living in this soulless, stupid place, waiting for something to happen. So I made something happen. And I've never felt so deadened, ever.'

'I feel tired, Steve, and as though I don't know you anymore. And you don't really know *me*.'

'I was selfish and stupid, Beth. I know. I get it. I wanted to put down the responsibility for a while. But it's still me. It's still me, loving you. Me for you. That's it. That's who I am.'

'But now *I* can't do it,' I shouted. 'I see how mistakes get made. How fragile everything is. And it scares the shit out of me. It's me that can't do it anymore.'

'Yes, you can, Beth. Don't give up.'

'There was a lot of silence in my house as a child. I can still hear it — that horrible, tight silence. I won't have it here.'

'I know. I don't want that either.'

'My mother can't talk anymore, not about anything real. It's been so long. And now there's so much ground to cover, it's just impossible. I don't want to end up like that.'

I needed to exorcise the memory of his infidelity, his night in that hotel, to set fire to it and watch it burn away to nothing. But I didn't think I could. So I knew something would always be changed now, with us.

'I know what I'm asking is a lot, honey.' He sucked in and went on. 'And I worry about the consequences of what I've done. I worry about what will happen further down the line: if you'll feel the need to balance things out, if there'll be something — *somebody* — else, you know, to even the score. In an odd way, it seems right that you should. Even though it makes me feel absolutely sick to even think that that might ever happen.'

He didn't know that I already had.

'Remember when Mae was born and everyone was so sad, so confused and sad?' He was standing right in front of me now with his jacket on. 'But they were happy too because it was a birth, a new life, a baby girl had been born. So they didn't know what to say. You remember?'

I nodded. 'So they said nothing. Or even worse, they said the wrong thing.' My voice was a whisper.

'Yes, but they didn't know it was the wrong thing, Beth. How could they? I see that now. I mean, I didn't say much that was right either. I burrowed myself down into the safety of my work, shut myself away from less certain things, from everyone really, and that included you. Most of all, from you.' He turned and looked at me. 'I've never told anyone this, Beth, but I had to pull over in the car when I was driving home from the hospital, that night she was born. On the side of an ugly street, I had to pull over I was crying so hard. I sat there for ages, crying for you. And for this little girl. And, I hate saying it, for myself. For a burden that I imagined. Because I didn't know either. I didn't know what Mae was or would be. Can you believe that I cried about having Mae in my life? I'm so ashamed of that. I never wanted you to know. I couldn't find the right words so I think I just stopped trying to talk. The confusion felt so complete, so deep and complete that it made me numb and I just didn't want to speak.' He rubbed his sleeve across his eyes. 'And you were in pain, of course, angry and hurt. And I used that — I used your anger as an excuse, to make it easier for me to turn away, to blame you for our problems.' He started to really cry now. 'I didn't know she'd be amazing. In every single way. So she's got forty-seven chromosomes. Big deal. For God's sake, she's the most well-adjusted person in this house.'

We both smiled.

'I still feel sad about it sometimes, Steve. I feel sad remembering that woman who gave birth to a lovely little girl but felt so much grief.' I sat on the edge of the bed looking at the floor, my jacket in a heap at my feet.

'I know you do. And I'm sorry I wasn't there enough, that I didn't try harder for you. I haven't felt at ease with the world since then, with where we are in it. I'm always waiting for someone to jump out from behind a door with bad news. I feel I can't rely on anything not happening anymore. Like everything is out of control and any amount of horrors are possible — are likely, even.'

I felt a rush of love listening to him. He'd been feeling it all too. Exactly as I did. Terror in the face of life. Circling the same thoughts, losing his mind in dread.

'I couldn't look into your eyes, Beth. I could see you were broken and it just reminded me of it. Of the pain I needed to ignore. Now, the possibility of *not* having Mae in my life is what I just can't consider. Of not being around her every day, here, at home with you, being her dad.'

I lifted my face and he hunkered down to

my level and looked straight at me.

He spoke quietly. 'You know that I feel I don't belong here, Beth, but I do belong with you. And if this is where you want to be, then this is where we'll be. Never stop loving me. I can live without anything else.'

Since Mae's birth, I could barely tolerate our life either. There was something unbearable in this place, Vesey Hill, something greedy and distasteful. Sometimes I could nearly taste it. It tasted bitter, like blood. Moirah and Anna ruling over the tractable cul-de-sacs.

I was crying now, crying for how we had failed each other for so long. For how I had known he was so unhappy, so lost; I had known it and I did nothing. For the silence, the layers of words unsaid, the anger, and the love held back.

'I saw that doctor about a month ago.' Steve's voice thickened. 'The one who told us he wouldn't have bet on her that first day.'

'Dr Burke.'

'Him. Burke. He was next in line to me at the shop, paying for his newspaper. I wanted to stuff it down his throat. I hate that bastard.'

How difficult it had been to try to get things right and how easy it had been to fail.

'You know, I prayed to my mother every

day we were apart. I prayed to her. And I remembered how she used to always tell me to go to mass, just before she hung up the phone. The last thing she'd say was, 'Go to mass, Stevie.' So for those weeks I did. I went to mass and prayed for us all to be together, in one house, one team. Can you believe that? Me at mass in the mornings.' He was laughing a little, tears streaming from his eyes. 'It took me too long to realise that you always had my back, Beth. But I knew it then because without you I could barely stand.'

While he spoke, I thought about the child I should have had those years ago, who would be an adult of twenty-six now. And how the worry that some God or the world would take Mae from me in exchange for the child that I took from the world gnawed at me at night.

'You're the apple of my eye, Beth Rogers; I just didn't fucking know it.'

And then we were holding each other, jagged pain and torrents of tears unleashing, time lurching as our bodies shuddered with sobs — letting feelings out, drawing each other back in.

What They Can Do

'After Mae has her operation,' Moirah's daughter locked her brown eyes on mine, 'will her Down syndrome be gone?'

'No, Chloe. It won't be gone, darling.'

'Will she be just the same, you know, as she is now?'

'Well, she'll have a healthier heart so she'll be fitter and stronger.'

'But she'll be . . . the same, as she is now?'

'Yes. Yes, she'll still be the same lovely Mae.' I smiled at her.

'Oh.'

★   ★   ★

It turned out that Mae did have one of 'those heart problems that they get'. And what had been born with her as a tiny leak had grown stealthily. Now, our daughter had a heart so big and stretched, it was the same size as mine.

And hers was heavy too.

The cardiac unit teemed with children with damaged and faulty hearts, none of them taller than my waist. Anguish piled on anguish, coating itself. I tried to swallow down a painful lump.

'You can't tell her. She won't understand. She's not capable of it, the poor mite.' My mother spoke.

'So you think we should ambush her?'

'It's not an ambush, Beth, if all the explaining in the world won't make a jot of difference.'

'You think we shouldn't even try to explain, that she doesn't deserve us to try to help her understand what's happening? You think that she won't want to go home?' I shook my head. 'I can't just shock her, Mum.'

'She has Down syndrome, Beth. And this is one of its many tragedies.' She refolded the dishcloth she had in her hands. 'And you're really setting me on edge with all of this, all this talk about explaining something when it just can't be done.'

Your sternum will be separated with a saw. Your ribs will be held apart with a metal grip. And you will be put on a heart-lung bypass machine, while a surgeon works on fixing the leaky valve in your heart. So that you won't die. You will wake up with drains coming from your very insides, intubating tubes in your airways, pacing wires stuck to the surface of your heart, and narrow tubes going into your neck. I will want to be with you every single second but I can't. I will be right outside, though, waiting for them to let me in, to let me back to you.

'You'll be able to run faster soon because you'll have a happy, strong heart,' I said to Mae that evening. 'And you'll have a cool scar down here,' I ran my finger the length of her chest, 'which will mean the doctor has finished, and you are all better. And Dada and I will be so proud of you for being such a brave girl.'

She understood the running faster.

* * *

Mae had rushed into the lift twenty-four hours before, taking her place at the panel, finger poised waiting to press the button.

'I do it?'

'Of course. Number 3,' Steve said.

She pressed it.

She smiled when the doors opened. Shouting 'Run fast!' our daughter skipped toward open-heart surgery.

* * *

Of course, it was foolish to think her heart had grown heavy because she knew she hadn't been fully loved from the start.

*　*　*

In a small airless room with the lights switched off, Mae sobbed and held both my hands while Steve kept her body still and the radiographer did an ECG.

Was it still a 'leak' when blood just flowed haphazardly, the wrong way, every way, with no bridges or boundaries or working dams? Blood out of control, free-flowing, and deathly.

The mouse clicked, the keyboard tapped, *click, tap tap, click, sob.*

I was falling. Falling, falling, Mae's trusting hands in mine, in this airless room. Falling, and no way to stop it. No end to it.

*　*　*

I had dressed up to leave for the hospital. If I didn't look tragic, if I looked like a capable mother expecting a successful outcome, and not a wrecked, devastated parent, then maybe devastating things — the most devastating thing — wouldn't happen.

When I came down the stairs, Steve was sitting in the garden with Mae on his lap, chasing nursery rhymes around her palm. He was wearing a new shirt.

Al said goodbye to Steve and me in the

kitchen. He came out to the car after us then and passed a photo in through the window to me. To put above Mae's bed for him until he was allowed to be with her again. He pressed his right hand flat against her window and she met it with hers on her side, flat, together, two starfish. His eyes damp. Not daring to say goodbye.

The photo was one of him on the couch with Mae looking up into his face, reading his features closely, her arms around his neck. Him smiling at her, so she could read his happiness. So she wouldn't worry. Caught up entirely in each other.

I watched him get small in the car wing mirror as we pulled away from the house. Only a week ago I'd told him about Mae's heart. He'd known there was something wrong the moment I came into his room and said, 'Hi!' too brightly. He'd pulled his earbuds from his ears and hit the little screen to pause it. His eyes wide as I spoke. Because he was able to understand, even the bits between the lines that I didn't say.

She would die in his lifetime. He wouldn't get away without it. Not now though, please not now.

★　★　★

'You won't have to worry about the cost of any of this, what you're facing. I don't want anyone worrying about the money. Private rooms, the best surgeon, whatever. It'll all be looked after.'

'Thanks, Dad, but that side of things is actually fine. The insurance will cover all of that and the surgeon is — '

'Even when I'm dead, I'll be paying for that child. And happy to do it.' He stayed swimming in his depth. 'She can count on that. I'll still be taking care of her financially, of what she needs. Even when I'm dead, I'll be doing it.'

★　★　★

'Kia Kaha, Beth. Kia Kaha, Steve. You will survive this, all of you together. I'll be thinking of you, and beautiful Mae and Al. Stay strong and be kind to each other.'

In those seconds between hanging up and the screen going blank, I saw Steve's dad lift the heels of his hands to his eyes and press down hard.

★　★　★

'You must be numb at this stage, what with all the bad news. It's just one thing after another for you.'

195

'Not really, Saoirse. This is the first challenge we've faced in a while.'

'I honestly don't know how you do it.'

'Well, Steve and I are doing our best to be positive about it.'

'Numb. You must be.'

'Actually, I wish I was.' I tried out a small laugh. 'I'm actually raw, I feel completely — '

'I've said it before, it's because you're such a coper. You just keep getting flattened by things. But you spring back up again! I don't know how you've any fight left.'

'Just putting one foot in front of the other, Saoirse.' Falling, falling. Resorting to clichés.

'There you go! You're just amazing. And with the shocking hand that life has dealt you.'

★ ★ ★

Steve stood and cleared his throat when Dr Daly walked into the room. In his late forties, small, and with serious features, he wore a suit and carried a briefcase. Competent. I stayed sitting on the bed with Mae, working on forgetting the darkness of the ECG with a safari-themed jigsaw. He leaned down and shook my hand by putting both of his around it, a gesture that was as grave as it was comforting. He spoke kindly to Mae, who regarded him closely and then looked away — back to the zebra pieces — having discerned enough.

I remembered overhearing Al tell my mother that if her way of helping was to pray, then at least some of her prayers should be for Dr Daly. And his hands.

In this small room, I could hear that his voice had wealth and certainty in it. It filled the air with explanations about severe regurgitation and significant risks and something about six to eight hours. Steve kept the nodding going, while Mae and I joined bits of zebras and pieces of elephants together.

Before he left, Dr Daly made a remark about us only having one choice — or maybe he said no choice — but it didn't matter which, because they're the same thing.

⋆ ⋆ ⋆

Six weeks earlier, waiting in his clinic, I'd seen a framed pencil sketch depicting him as a wizard. And under it — 'Thank you for my life. Isobel, May 2011.' It's almost all I can remember of that afternoon.

⋆ ⋆ ⋆

'OK now, Mammy, are we ready?' A middle-aged nurse with a clear voice stood over me. 'I'm going to take you to the ICU to see a child that had a similar surgery to Ismae just yesterday so you'll have an idea how she'll look when she comes out. So you won't get a fright. It can be easier to see the bits and bobs for the first time when they're on a child that isn't your own.'

'OK. Yes. That sounds good.' I could do this. Prepare myself to be better, for Mae.

Steve squeezed my hand and nodded as I left with her.

The ICU doors had codes and bells and permissions to be sought and then there was waiting, scrubbing-in and aprons and protective hair coverings. The regular bustle of the hospital's lifts and corridors gave way to metallic light, an aggressive beeping-silence, and heady chemical smells. A large sign on the wall permitted that only plain wedding bands be worn.

We stood next to a large metal cot, but I kept looking straight ahead.

'Now, please God, Ismae will look something like this tomorrow evening.'

Don't look down. You will only fall if you look down. Find a point on the wall and don't look down.

'I have a note for over her bed — I typed it last night — listing little things she likes and also noises and sounds that scare her. Just for the staff to know. Do you think they would

198

mind me leaving it? Maybe sticking it up for me? Just until I'm allowed in.' The words dribbled from me, falling out onto the floor.

'Of course.'

'Will the nurses know to cover her hands with the little cut-off socks that I brought? Just to hide the cannulas and plasters from her, if that's OK? She won't like looking at them. I didn't think about the drains and the wires and how to hide those, really. But I have her headphones so she won't hear the alarms going off and — '

The nurse touched me on the arm and spoke more gently than she had. 'Whatever you need.'

'She has Down syndrome — they mightn't notice when her eyes are closed — and it means that she won't really know what's happening. And they mightn't understand her speech.' Hot tears streamed into the well around my nose, onto my lips. 'And I have a photo of her brother that she might like having near her.'

'The nurses will take good care of her. I promise you.'

'I know, I know they will. I'm sorry. I just don't know what I can do, what's the best thing to do. I bought her new nightdresses but I'm thinking that she won't need them, that it was silly of me, that she — '

'No, she will be without any clothes for some time. So we can keep an eye on her, her drains and her wound and so we can access anything — if a situation arose whereby . . . '

I nodded and my tears fell into the child's cot.

Don't look down.

'As she comes around, she may be a bit withdrawn from you, you know, a bit cool toward you. The children with Down's are often confused and distant. Not all of them, mind. But quite a few. If you know this now it won't come as a shock though.'

Falling, falling. *Find a point on the wall.*

'We will also need you and your husband to sign life-support consent this evening so . . . '

I felt her strong arm around my back as the words bleached away.

★ ★ ★

'Hello, I'm Ismae's nurse for tonight. I'm Emma.' A tall, young nurse with a swingy ponytail of blonde hair stood at the end of Mae's bed, smiling.

Steve smiled back and stood up to shake her hand. I felt a twinge of something, a pain. I leaned over the bed and brushed Mae's hair from her forehead. She was sleepy, exhausted by the day.

'So what time will they send for her in the morning?' I already knew the answer but wanted to let the air out of both their smiles, remind them why we were here.

I watched Mae's heartbeat and her oxygen saturations on the monitors while the nurse answered. Then Steve asked something about fasting and the pre-op routine, things we had already been through.

I got into the bed beside my daughter and pulled the metal railing up behind me. I fitted myself around the curve of her back and put my arm over her chest, over her big heart. My head on the plastic pillow, I pulled the washed-away blue blanket up over us and felt her drift off against me.

★   ★   ★

Walking through a hospital late at night, everyone scans each other's faces for signs of anything — distress, relief, sorrow, energy. The teenage girl with cerebral palsy and the dyed blue hair; the boy in the bandages whose skin weeps even where it is uncovered; the little girl in the wheelchair with the paint-spattered hubcaps; the exhausted-looking doctor with the freckles; the night porter with the plaster over his eyebrow — the kind that hides a piercing but also draws attention to it; my husband with his smile, his handshake, his thank you; and Emma, our nurse tonight, with her tiny diamond in her nose, which glints when it catches the light.

We passed the café, all locked up and shuttered. We'd sat in there this afternoon with my mother. She had her back to the café, facing a wall so as not to see 'the mishmash of little broken bodies about the place'.

Steve had reached forward with a hospital leaflet.

'This might be helpful for you, Johanna, to give you an idea of what's happening. So you can understand Mae's surgery and her recovery.'

'Oh, Steve! I couldn't read that.' She recoiled. 'Those things are way too upsetting for me. I don't like to even *hear* about sad things like that.'

★ ★ ★

The parents' accommodation was on the fourth floor, with no lift to it. A few pot plants scattered along the hallway sucked the last of the air out. Our room had a Catholic look about it: dark shiny-varnished furniture, heavy patterned curtains parted and tied at the sides, greying window nets, a brown

202

carpet and two narrow single beds. Because parents in a children's hospital have more on their minds. Padre Pio looked down from the walls, gentle eyes and mean eyebrows.

The oval mirror on the wall was exactly the same as one from my old bedroom, one that still hung there. Seeing it, here, gave me a flicker of something comforting, a small feeling of destiny. That this was somewhere I was meant to be. But then, I'd never felt particularly at home, at home. I looked into its glass and saw I looked wretched, my face drawn, my outfit all wrong and shouting. How many thousands of defeated faces this mirror must have shown. I couldn't bear to think of them, all the faces its memory held.

I could see Steve reflected behind me. Taking his shirt off, his broad back filling the mirror's width. I craved him, his strength and the bulk of him. Now, to lift my pain off my shoulders, to set it to the side just for a short while.

But he repelled me too. He might crush me.

I imagined him looking at the nurse, taking her in. Smiling, baring his teeth. I sat down on my bed, and it made a plastic sound from somewhere amongst its thin sheets and blanket. Steve laughed. 'They certainly don't want us to feel too spoiled, do they?' and he started to unpack our case.

I could feel the same rigidness about me as I did when he went away overnight for business lately. Hyper-alert to changes in the house, to the light fading, to small sounds, to the clock in the darkness, as though I'd left the keys in the front door or a bomb ticking on the stairs.

I watched him carefully unfold our clothes and use up all three of the wire hangers clanging in the musty press on mine. Everything sorted, he sat on his bed and smiled at me — *ta dah!* A memory came up through me and I saw him sitting on a different bed, in another room, across from me, before. Framed by the edges of a laptop screen, smiling then too, he had been a picture.

I must've winced because here, in this place, he leaned forward and said, 'We must be strong, honey. For her.'

I could feel sweat prickling under my arms. Anger and need were twitching, competing.

'That nurse seems nice.' My voice was all shards.

'I thought so,' he said, wary. 'Did you not?'

I hunched my shoulders up and breathed deeply. *Shrug.*

'I'm sure Mae will like her, but I'd rather get back down there myself,' he said, putting on a fresh shirt.

I'll bet.

'In case she wakes up.'

I whispered the words out — 'I've watched you and her a million times, in my mind's eye. You and Jane. And in my version, in my eyes, she is blonde and tall. And young. Like that nurse.'

I sounded pathetic, I was pathetic, I am pathetic. Fuck, it still hurt though. Him and Jane. It still fucking hurt. Even in a situation such as this. Or perhaps because of it.

I went on, my voice sinking to almost nothing, a barely audible tangle of sounds and raggedy feelings.

'Our little girl is having her heart opened in a matter of hours. And instead of being with her, I'm up here with you falling apart because I don't want you to go back down. I don't want you down there. With that nurse, with *Emma*.'

Steve's face looked slapped.

'Is that why you were so short with her? I thought it was just the stress of everything. Oh, Beth.' He sat down next to me on my bed.

'My father said I must forgive you, you know, back then.'

He nodded.

'And I thought I had. I really did, Steve. But then something like this happens — ' I

motioned at the room, the hospital outside it
— 'something fucking *hard*, where I really
need you, and I feel it again. I need
something solid now to steady me, to stop me
from fraying into nothing, and you're not — I
just, I'm afraid to let . . . ' I looked down at
the threadbare carpet and life felt like a
climb.

I remembered my father's words. *It's
simply what must be done*. What would he
know about forgiveness or the utter brutality
of loving another person? Nobody ever
fucking upset him. He did all the upsetting,
made all the choices, felt nothing.

'What can I do, Beth? We've been through
this. I don't know what to say. What do you
need from me?'

'I don't know, Steve. I'm not even looking
for joy or expecting great happiness anymore,
I'm really not. I just want to be rid of the
pain. All the different pains that I can't even
differentiate between now.' My voice swam
through the room. 'But I can't lean into you.'

'You can. Oh, you can, Beth. I've told you
— I choose us, you and me, and Al and Mae.
It's what I want. You and me.' He cast about
the tiny room for some proof of what he was
saying. 'It wasn't just me that took us down,
Beth. You put me out of your reach too after
Mae was born, for so long. I'm sorry for what

I did but it wasn't just my mistake.' He tilted my chin gently so I could look at him as he spoke. 'You know that, honey. We have hurt each other. But now we're together; I'm home and we're trying to build our way back up again, but you're still keeping yourself apart. You have to choose. Do you choose me?'

'I want to.' I spoke carefully. 'Now, more than ever, because nobody loves Mae as you and I do, and we're standing on this cliff together. But I can't believe that you will hold us. Not just right now, during these worried hospital days, but always.'

I wanted to believe in him, in his body, in his body being mine. Only mine.

'So much has been lost, Steve. Our life, our family, our health. I just, I just don't — I mean, there are bits and edges of it still there but in scraps, in an impossible pile. And I have to sift through it all to find what's worth keeping, the bits that still shine, that are worth gluing.' I held my hands out, for him to see the pile, to see the impossibility of the task. He looked at my hands. 'And he saw. And then something else shit happens and I have to start sifting again.'

'But love fixes things. It repairs itself. Beth, it does.' He put his hands up to my face. 'Listen to me. *It does*. Love repairs.'

His eyes were dark and reflective like pools of polished stone.

'I can't lose her. I just can't. Too much has been lost already. Too much of *me*. Nearly everything I do now is — it's just *irrelevant*. There's no substance to it. Mae is the biggest demand on me, but she's my purpose too. I know that. And I'm sorry that I've fought it. I will fade away if she leaves me.'

I lay back on the bed, my eyes dry and closed to everything.

'Do you think she's frightened?' My voice cracked.

'I think she's probably confused.'

And I cried then, because I hadn't been able to do anything about that. I hadn't been able to reach her thoughts, to climb over the walls around her mind, to relate what was happening in a way that she could understand. She was three and a half years old and she was flying blind. And she had no choice.

★ ★ ★

The sky was a bruise. Murky blues leached away into slates and grey-yellows. Steve and I pulled up at a small park near the hospital. We watched people pass the car, the threatened rain making them determined in their strides. But we had nowhere to be.

I knew we would always remember what we did during these hours. What we did while our daughter's sternum was being sawn apart so that hands could get to the core of her, to save her.

Steve took a small creased brown paper bag from his pocket. 'Any idea what might be in here?' he asked as he unfurled it. 'I haven't worn this jacket since, oh, I don't know, probably since the last funeral we went to. Whenever that was.' A thick silence crept into the car and hung between us.

'Oh, they're cough sweets,' he said a moment later, as the sticky mess revealed itself. 'Want one?' and he passed me what looked like a miniature ale-brown glass ashtray.

'Come on. Have it and let's get out.'

He connected his earbuds to his phone and put one in his ear, passing me the other. Taking my hand, he found a gate and walked me into the small, square park, which had a nondescript stone monument in its centre. It had been defaced by graffiti.

'This is a really fucking terrible place, Steve.'

'It has a certain charm. Shabby shit,' he said as he put his phone into his pocket and squeezed my hand.

And then Nick Cave's voice came in like a haunting, filling my ear, filling the air, filling all the spaces between things, between us, and it was a moment of such unexpected *feeling* that I stopped thinking, thinking and just walked.

> *I don't believe in an interventionist God*
> *But I know, darling, that you do*
> *But if I did I would kneel down and ask Him*
> *Not to intervene when it came to you*
> *Not to touch a hair on your head*
> *To leave you as you are*
> *And if He felt He had to direct you*
> *Then direct you into my arms*
> *Into my arms, O Lord*
> *Into my arms, O Lord*

So we walked, holding hands and sharing earphones in a shitty park that we would never visit again, while the skies darkened further and the rain and the music poured down upon us.

Our hearts in ribbons.

★　★　★

I supposed I should let my parents know, let people know, that Mae was in surgery now.

Time had dragged its heels since dawn. The anaesthetist had lines around his eyes, the rest of his face hidden by a mask. Mae's eyes dropped and he carefully let her head fall back onto the table.

'Goodbye now, Mum and Dad,' he said in a voice that jarred, too loud.

Steve gave him a short, firm nod. His eyes red-rimmed and wide.

I kissed her head. Steve just stood, staring.

And then — 'Bring her back to me,' he almost shouted.

★ ★ ★

An older lady sat silently in the front row, offering her face up to the crucifix like a plea. Beside her, a man muttered well-worn prayers.

Curtains hung on each side of the altar. For what? It was just a table, really, with the candle on it. Were they there to hide it? There would be nothing, if it was hidden. Nothing behind it. Nothing in front. Just plastic chairs. The hospital chapel was bare and sterile, but it felt appropriate. An honourable place to wait as the evening collapsed into night.

I was making every promise to something in the sky when my phone buzzed quietly. Trying to get to my feet, trying to feel my legs, trying to get out by the chairs, I answered it.

Steve watched my face.

The ICU nurse asked us to please come to the second floor and wait at the blue seats for Dr Daly.

* * *

I overheard a young mother of about twenty-eight gently tell her father that her son, his grandson, Max, did, after all that, have the cancer.

The older man's hands went to his hair and he slid down the wall.

'Little Max, little Max.'

She slid down so she could meet his eyes.

'But it's the kind of cancer that has a very good survival rate.'

He nodded slowly, his eyes taking in hers.

'Forty to sixty per cent,' she said, nodding slowly, keeping his tempo.

'I wouldn't call that very good,' he said.

Their foreheads tilted forward and met each other, ashen.

I turned away. The feeling I had had recently when traffic gridlocked around Vesey Hill for the first time ever that I can recall, an ambulance visible up ahead, inside the gates, blocking the entrance to our street. A police car racing past leaving me in the traffic behind it. Hurriedly punching Steve's number into my phone — please answer, please answer, please God, let him answer, please let it not be her. Dread, waiting for delight, dread, waiting for the phone to be lifted. Waiting.

And now again, dread and delight beat each other, wrestled with each other, frantic.

'How long have we been here?' Steve sat back down.

I checked the time. 'Almost fifteen minutes.'

I stared at the floor. Industrial tiles, one black, one white, one black, one white. The kind that are flat and shiny and meet each other with precision. Non-porous and with no room between for grout. So blood and vomit and tears couldn't gather.

And then, footsteps. Through the balustrade a short man wearing scrubs and carrying a briefcase was coming up the stairs. I nudged Steve but he was already on his feet, looking.

'Beth, Steven,' Dr Daly said. Neither of us spoke.

'I would consider it a pretty good repair,' he said.

His smile and the way he stood, square and proud, said more than his words.

'It worked?' Steve grabbed him by the hand and shook it. Up and down, up and down. Taking water from a well.

'Yes, 'it worked'. It worked very well

213

indeed.' A warm, generous smile.

Steve blew out a relieved sound and started to wipe away tears. He clasped me. All of me, into him.

'Beth, he saved her life.' He turned back to Dr Daly. 'Thank you, Doctor. Thank you. We can't ever — I mean, you must hear this every day.'

'Not every day. Some days I hear very different things. But this is a good day. I'm delighted for you both and for your daughter.'

I closed my eyes then as he explained the procedure, how the repair had gone, what would be required in terms of her recovery, how long it would take, just how much her little body had been through.

Mae would live.

'I thought I would lose her,' I said. 'I thought she would be taken from me.'

'Not today, Mrs Rogers,' he said, and he turned and walked away.

★　★　★

The first thing you saw were the three drains. One on each side of her chest and one in the centre, thick drains like clear garden hoses emptying hay-coloured fluid, dark fat from her insides, into Perspex boxes at the base of the bed. Lines and tubes coming from everywhere. Little ties on her wrists. To stop her pulling where there was pain, where there was fear, pulling to get out past her confusion. Little ties so she could live. And a scar. A slash running the full length of her torso, the mark of a knife wound, splitting her in half. Marking her out again. Her face and now her body too.

And, oh, that face, her face under it all, swollen and rounder than usual. Her mouth open and so dry it was covered in a thick crystallised layer of ooze and broken skin.

Her eyes. The only part of her unchanged. Her tiny half-moons shut to the world, shut to me. Would they see me differently when they opened? In my head I told her what was happening, why it had to happen, how I adored her, just her as she is, how she would always be my piano.

Mae flat and motionless. She could've been dead but the monitors said she wasn't.

I recognised an old feeling, the one I'd had in the first weeks after her birth. I wanted to know the final result, the outcome, without living through the time it takes to get there.

'Can I touch her?'

'Yes, but lightly and not on the chest or abdomen. Maybe just on her arm.'

I touch it, lightly, and it is warm. She is alive. And she is warmer even than before, I think. I want to scoop her up, avoid pressing her delicate little ribs and their broken cage. I want to scoop her up and run.

Everywhere readings and beeping and outputs and watching and noting. And then I see the little gloves I made out of the new rainbow socks to cover her cannula, so she wouldn't see it and be frightened. They are on her hands, as I had asked, but they cover so little. Almost nothing. And, seeing my foolishness, my ineptitude, my *lack of understanding* of this — of all of this enormity — so plain in front of me, makes me lose my footing then completely and I step backwards into my husband.

'We're changing shift shortly so you will have to leave.'

I want to stay. But I want to be carried away.

★ ★ ★

Mae opened her eyes and stared. At the ceiling, and then at as much of the room as her angle in the cot and her medication would allow.

She closed them again. She mustn't have seen me.

★ ★ ★

Mae opened her eyes and stared. At the ceiling, and then at me.

She tried to make a sound. But there were tubes and restriction and pain.

'Oh, my love,' and I leaned my face over her face, over her eyes and her dry mouth, and I touched her bloated cheek and I smiled, smiled to reassure her, so she knew she was safe, it was safe to love me.

She tried to swallow, then closed her eyes again.

All down her chest, the two sides of her scar are raised, meeting in a point. A ridge. Like a long, narrow mountain range. Both jagged sides bound together where they meet, but repelling each other and falling away too. I want to run my hand along it, to feel this raw seam holding my child together, keeping all the bits inside. But I'm not allowed to.

★   ★   ★

Steve sits on a chair while the nurse undoes Mae's wrists, gathers and untangles all the wires and tubes and drains, and scrapes the hateful Perspex box along the ground so she can be passed to him, to sit upright for a few moments.

I watch him, the surety of his arms, his solid body holding Mae and her patchwork

217

one. His face has an awed satisfaction, seeing the drains fill with yellowy fat as he holds her.

'Dada.' A whisper.

'Mae, darling.'

'Home?'

A tear runs from the side of her left eye.

'Yes. Very soon.'

'Better.'

'Yes, when you're feeling better. And we will run fast, Mae, the two of us. Run fast together.'

Her eyes close again.

I hear his breathing, the very life of him, as he sits there, capable. I'd know it was him anywhere by the sound of his breathing. How much of me now is part of him? How much of me is what I have become from being with him? We two can't be parted. We three.

That night in my narrow bed on the fourth floor, I watch my husband sleep while our daughter is downstairs being kept alive, being kept asleep, being kept apart from this world, draining from the inside out. His face is tense, his brow furrowed, his dark features darker even than ever, but beautiful.

He turns and opens his eyes and reaches out across the gap between our beds. We hold hands there, our arms suspended, a bridge over the floor.

'Never go.' His voice is quiet.
'I won't.'

$$\star \quad \star \quad \star$$

The parents' kitchen is not a place of sharing. Identical boxes of teabags are lined up, all open, all the same but for the different room numbers scrawled on their sides, labelled milk, almost-empty biscuit packets with family names on sticky labels. Nothing is shared, neither things nor stories. Everything too tense, too precious.

From where I stand now waiting for the kettle to boil, the view is of the back of an old disused part of the hospital with exposed, snaking pipework and dark windows, paint peeling from everywhere.

A couple sit opposite each other on the black leather couches here, in this kitchen — parents of a heart child. She sits forward and says something as she tidies her chocolate wrapper into an empty cup. He is speaking into his phone. She puts her jacket on and picks her bag up off the floor. Which takes his attention from his phone for a moment. He hangs up then and they speak quietly, impatient with each other. I boil the kettle again. Steve looks for our box of teabags in the line.

Then the man's phone rings again, almost immediately. And he answers it. Which surprises the woman, and I find I'm surprised too.

She sighs noisily, even over the sound of the kettle, and leaves the room. Days spent here are fraught.

I stare at the four coasters on the sideboard in front of me. They are of four obvious, international landmarks: Sydney Opera House, the Eiffel Tower, and the Statue of Liberty. Much of the picture on the fourth one has peeled off to reveal the pale cork below but from the corner that remains, I take it to be the Golden Gate Bridge. I've been to all four places. All before Mae was born.

It will be time to push on soon, when we get out of here, high time to get on with things, with Mae. We need updating. I need updating. My position in my own life and in my marriage.

Steve sees me looking at the coasters. He lifts his arm beside me and in one motion he gathers me in and with his other hand loops my hair behind my ear.

So many peculiar changes from enchantment to disenchantment and then back again, from joy to anger to joy, from terror to a kind of contentment and then back to fear, sweeping through our life together like a current, sometimes wiping everything away and other times rising and delivering us back to dry land, restoring us to safety in a single movement.

★ ★ ★

Drains and tubes and wires move every time Mae shifts in the bed or when she sits up to try to eat. Climbing down to walk to the toilet is a marathon for her but it's as important as it is difficult. That much she can understand. 'Then home?'

'Yes, darling, soon.'

She doesn't want help. She wants to be a big girl again.

'Keep the drains low! Lower than her body!' a passing nurse barks a reminder. 'Or the fluids will seep back into her and we don't want that, do we?'

'We certainly don't!' Steve shouts back cheerfully, and then rolls his eyes. We are in Room 7 now, back on the ward. And I'm keeping it tidy, being good to it so it will be good to us.

Mae's big heart is shrinking, shrinking back underneath the red ridge that climbs up from beneath the neckline of her nightdress, like a medal that can't ever be taken off. It will grow with her body, always drawing the eye, always speaking for her.

A group of seven young medical students came in this morning, before she was dressed. And the first question asked after a little silence —

'Did you know when you were pregnant that she had Down syndrome?'

'No, I didn't.' I smiled.

After another little silence, that student spoke again — 'I'm sorry.'

I'm sorry. Steve and I had met a lot of people who were sorry, since Mae was born. And every time, those two words made it hard to believe, hard to pretend, that nothing bad had happened.

The student looked back at Mae. And then — 'Isn't it amazing, though? What they can do?'

'It really is,' I said.

Just for a moment, I allowed myself to see through his young eyes. A little girl with stitches hanging from her like Frankenstein's monster, a large patch covering the unthinkable hole knitting together on her neck, thick rubber tubes draining fat from her insides and an angry slash down her body where she had been split in two. Oh, but more than this. A profoundly disabled little girl with a limited vocabulary and a limited mind, who would always be dependent, always a child. But now, macabre too.

Isn't it amazing, though? What they can do. *Even for a child such as this.*

I felt Steve behind me, his arms low slung around my waist. And I leaned into him.

⋆ ⋆ ⋆

'THERE SHE IS!' Al comes through the door bringing something of the outside air and light with him. 'Mae, you big legend. I've missed you so much.' He sounds older, louder, *capable*. And my eyes fill for the sheer and gorgeous fact of him. The clear and open normality he carries into this serious room of quiet caution. My son. Playing the character of the worldly older brother in a play.

Mae leans forward a little, her arms stretched out — 'AL!' It's as loud a word as I've heard from her since she skipped out of the lift that morning ten days ago.

'You brave, brave girl. Look at these hoses! What's going on here?' and he leans down for her hug, gently but fully.

'Drains, silly!' Steve corrects him, making a funny face at Mae, who gives a little giggle. Another first.

'DRAINS!' she says loudly.

'They're cool. You look like an octopus! I'll bet they're annoying too, though, huh? You'll be glad to get them out.'

'She is doing so well, they'll be gone really soon. No more drains. Very soon.' Steve kisses the top of her head.

Mae smiles. Proud of her drains, for the first time, for just a moment.

'Well, Granny and Grandad are just parking the car and then they're coming straight up to see you, you big hero.'

My son turns to me then and speaks more quietly.

'So is her Down's gone, or what? Did they manage to chase it out of her?' He gives my shoulder a squeeze and sits next to me, looks at me. His eyes full of knowing, so much more than his fifteen years. *How are you, Mum?*

★ ★ ★

I hear my mother's voice in the corridor and look up to see her interrogating a nurse. The nurse takes Mae's chart from the wall outside the room, and they appear to be discussing it in great detail.

My mother dabs at her hair and leans on the door handle, pushing it through quite dramatically. She is fully in the room now, clicking her tongue and managing still to flurry, despite having run out of floor space. The air in the room shifts.

Mae is the first to speak: 'Granny.'

'Oh, my angel, my little Ismae.' My mother leans over and quickly pats Mae's hand. 'Look at all of this carry-on.' She motions at the wires and monitors. 'What a lot of upset and nonsense! The nurse just told me you have the strongest heart in all of Ireland. And no mistake!' She widens her eyes at me as she lowers herself into the visitor's chair near the door, letting me know that the nurse is an imbecile.

My father is at the door now, his hip having given my mother her chance to get ahead. And she is back up on her feet when she sees him.

'Here — have my chair, Dermot, darling.'

'Mae, Mae, Daisy Mae.' He ignores my mother and goes straight to the bed and sits sideways onto it, his voice soft and reassuring. If he notices the horrors and sounds of the medical paraphernalia he doesn't show it. And yet, it's almost all there is.

'Mae, sweetheart, you're the bravest person I know.' He has always had a particular smile that he bestows when he's impressed by someone. Wide and certain. He bestows it now. Mae has impressed him and it makes me even more proud of her. He is a tough crowd.

'Grandad.'

'Yes, my love. It's Grandad.'

'I've spoken to the nurse,' my mother declares from the corner, 'and everything seems to be going as well as we could have hoped.'

My father turns to me. 'Let her take her time now, whatever she needs. Whatever you need.'

'We're in no hurry,' Steve says.

My father nods. 'And nothing else matters now. Just this little girl here. Whatever bills there are, just let me know. And I can sit with her all day, if that's what's best.'

'Well, with your hip, you really shouldn't, Dermot,' comes from the corner.

My father's phone rings in his coat pocket. He answers it quickly. 'Dermot O'Connor.'

Pause.

'Yes, OK. I see.'

Pause.

'Not really.'

Pause.

'Mmm. Later then.'

Pause.

'I'll call you.' He stabs at the red button and then turns his phone off.

'Who was that?' my mother asks, airily.

'John. Wondering if I wanted to play tomorrow.'

My mother shifts in the plastic chair and turns her earring. I don't believe him either.

★ ★ ★

Three black crosses, each made of lines of coarse knots, will replace Mae's drains the next morning, her insides running clear and drying up, the box louder now, whirring empty. Strong stitches pulling the holes in tight. Black crosses at the end of the long, red mountain range.

Her body a map, her face still a sign.

★ ★ ★

Mae is asleep. Tucked inside me curled in a crescent on her bed, no drains left to keep her cautious, to keep her body flattened, to disturb the quiet. Steve sits to the side, his left arm across us, holding us together, his head on my shoulder.

A dark spell has been broken; Mae's heart has done it. Love repairs.

★ ★ ★

'And remember: don't bath her! Her incisions can't be submerged for weeks!'

'The Rogers are leaving.' Steve gives a little final salute to the staff, his voice filled with protection.

'Ladies — ' He takes Mae's hand and

mine, one of us on each side. Leaving here now, with her.

Oh, and the relief of being outside with her fills everything. It sings in the air. Even our car seems different, better, tidier, and the doors heavier, like we've just borrowed it. Mae is so happy — 'Go home!' — to be out, to be free, to be safe in her car seat, my old Cabbage Patch doll with the chopped-off fringe in her lap. She is still wearing the little sock-gloves, covering only bruises now. But she wants to keep them on.

Steve's smile, his hand on my knee between gear changes, the lovely weight of our pauses between words and kisses. And I feel him like a want in me.

When we park on our cobblelocking, Al comes out onto the step and waves both arms at Mae, side to side, like he is directing a plane. She laughs a great, full laugh. I look up at our house, the force of it, and it feels like somewhere we used to live. Not a place for much longer, not a place for us.

★   ★   ★

Mae and I, side by side, brushing our teeth. More important than ever now to keep her heart well.

Brush, brush, brush.

She is brushing, her little head turned, face serious, watching me, copying.

I watch us both in the mirror.

Foam, smiling, brush, brush.

The top of her scar peeks up over her neckline where we will always see the joins. Her triumph.

What they can do.

★ ★ ★

We sit in the back garden that first night back, Steve and I. Al and Mae are in their beds and it's late, but mild enough for us to eat out there if we keep the patio heater on. Sommer had left food for us with a bottle of wine and a note — 'A good heart these days is hard to find. x'

As he walks by the back of my chair, carrying our empty plates to the kitchen, Steve leans down and kisses my cheek. Just passing. As though its nothing.

I throw my head back, stretch my legs out straight in front of me, and look up at the still night sky and the few stars stubborn against it. I count four. Four of us held together. Bound. With tonight and tomorrow and another tomorrow ahead of us, not just a parade of gaping hours but opportunities.

And a wave of something familiar but long-forgotten rises within me: the feeling of being lucky.

The Lighthouse

The wind flattened Steve's shirt against his chest.

He gathered a few pebbles into his palm and one by one sliced them long and straight so they skimmed the surface out where the water was dark and deep — once, twice, three times — before sinking so the waves could carry them back to him again.

'I can't remember the last time I was on a beach,' I said, as I took two little wrapped parcels from my bag.

Steve came over and sat down next to me.

'For me?' he asked as I handed him the one with the S on the paper.

'It's just a bagel — with the fillings you like and no cream cheese.'

'Carefully wrapped in some pretty paper. And no cream cheese. I love it. Thank you.' And he leaned in and kissed me on the forehead.

We ate in silence looking out at the waves.

'So what now?' I said after we'd finished.

'We'll go home and I'll make you some tea in your favourite blue cup and you'll smile at me. And I'll smile back. And then, as you

Irish say, we'll be away.' He stood up and brushed the sand off his hands, then reached for mine to pull me to my feet. 'If you really want to, I suppose we could go to bed for the afternoon.'

I considered this for a minute. 'OK.'

★ ★ ★

As we walked back to the car, he told me about his memories of the beach where he grew up: of the hot bright days; of the smells of the ocean right there before him, first thing in the morning and last thing at night — not an angry, slatey sea that people drive to on a Sunday afternoon but a real, living thing to be part of and to feel, every day.

I really listened to him as he spoke this time, feeling his pleasure. He was drying up here, ageing. I could hear it. Like a frog forced to live only on dry land.

'My times at home, my memories of being there are like lights spaced out along a string. They sustain me. I think about us living there, the four of us, all of the time.'

'I know.'

He didn't know that I was thinking about it too. I would protect this love. I would gather it up and protect it. I wanted my family together now — my husband and my children

— in a place where our world would be less confined, less boxed in. Where we could wring some joy and freedom from this life.

He twirled me and I laughed. I had thought it would take more time and effort and some diligence to love Steve back again, to really love him, but it didn't. I put my head against his chest and he held me close. Love repairs.

⋆   ⋆   ⋆

We went home that day and he took my hand, leading me up the stairs. And then kisses and more kisses pressed into each other, breaths quickened, time slowed, our legs and bodies damp and tangled. Moving slowly, then faster, lips apart. We were comfortable, uninhibited with each other. His face, his openness, his mistakes, my mistakes; it was Steve and me, and it was enough.

Later, we lay side by side, hands entwined, staring at the ceiling; two starfish.

Agnes

I saw Agnes before she saw me. She was propped up on a straight-backed chair between her bed and a window. A steel tray with claw sides was gripped over the chair's arms, right up against her middle, keeping her from falling forward. There was nothing on the tray but a small bowl full of tired-looking grapes. Her jaw was hanging so her mouth sat open. As I came toward her, her face tilted up and she pulled her lips together, smiled and straightened herself.

'Beth.' Her voice was stronger than I expected.

I looked around for another chair but there was none so I bent my legs to bring our faces level.

'Grandma,' I said quietly.

'Get up, girl. I don't want you kneeling before me. I'm not dead yet. I'd rather we both stand,' she bellowed.

She started to shift impatiently in the chair so I quickly stood and unclasped the tray.

She farted three times as she got herself up and onto her feet, one for each jerky move-ment as her brittle old form righted itself.

She was upright now but had gained very little height. Seated behind the tray, she'd been able to hide how tiny she'd become.

'I think it might be best if we both get onto the bed, Grandma. Maybe? You could rest back on the pillows and I'll sit up beside you.'

She sighed and offered me her hand. Her nails had hard ridges running down them and were painted a peachy-silver colour. When her feet left her slippers behind on the floor, I noticed the knuckles of her toes had black and wiry hairs sticking up out of them. She wouldn't like people noticing those.

'What are you still doing here, anyway?' she said as I helped her to hoist herself onto the bed.

'I've only just arrived. I came to see you.'

'I know that! Sure didn't I just watch you walk in? I don't mean *here*.' She motioned around the room with her stiff arm. 'I mean HERE. In Ireland. You should be long gone to New Zealand with your husband before it's too late. There's nothing you want here.'

She looked into my face as she shuffled into the centre of the bed.

'You know I'm right.'

I nodded and covered her feet and legs in the light sheet.

In the next bed, an old man was drinking out of a plastic lidded beaker. Between sips

235

he noisily cleared his throat. Agnes tutted loudly at him.

I took a photograph of Al and Mae out of my purse to show her.

'She's emancipated, God bless her,' he shouted at me, side-nodding at Agnes, his hand over one half of his mouth so she might not hear his roars. 'So thin.'

I tried not to laugh. Agnes rolled her eyes.

'She's losing weight at a fierce rate. Fiery still, though. Are you her daughter?' Thin, milky spittle flew from his mouth with the words.

'No, I'm her granddaughter.'

'And this is my *great*-granddaughter and my *great*-grandson.' Agnes turned and spoke to him with a proud voice. She passed the photograph back to me to show him. He squinted and leaned forward as though trying to divine any form at all from the picture wobbling between his liver-spotted hands.

'Very nice,' he said at last, nodding. He looked at me. 'She's a grand, stout young girl.' Up close, I saw he had a round face and kind, watery eyes, like a grandfather in a child's picture book.

'Yes, thank you,' Agnes snapped. She pointed toward him so I would take the photograph back.

The barred window next to her bed looked

out onto the roof of the A&E unit. A plastic Tesco bag lay trapped on the jagged edge of a broken slate.

'Are you admiring the view, darling?' I recognised my mother's forced jolly tone as she arrived into the room.

I turned and my father gave me a little salute before commandeering the only chair.

'Oh, Dermot, look. What a sunset. From here, it actually looks marvellous. Come and see. You'd enjoy it.'

'You've seen one sunset, you've seen them all,' he said, unfolding a newspaper that lay on the side table. 'Isn't that right, Aggie?' He winked at her.

Agnes nodded and let out a harsh laugh, like a crow.

'I'll just change the water in this vase.' My mother carried a mass of lilies to the sink on the other side of the room.

'Well? How do you think she looks?' My grandmother leaned in and whispered, gesturing toward my mother.

'Who?'

'Your mother. Who else? What's eating her? She's looking worse every day.'

Agnes seemed to be reversing their patient-visitor roles.

'She looks fine. She's OK, I think.'

'Come now, Beth. She looks shocking.

237

Something's killing her. If she's not actually sick, then it's something else. Probably your bloody father. Don't tell me you can't see it.' She sat back. And then leaned forward again. 'Although, you don't look great yourself, actually. You'd want to get out of here. You're not as young as you think.'

Now, I didn't know where she meant — the hospital, the country?

My mother's shoes came clack-clacking back across the room with the flowers.

'But Mummy's furniture — now *that* was beautiful,' Agnes said more loudly, moving on from our exchange. 'And how she did her hair. All up in a knot.' She piled her own few wispy hairs on top of her head to demonstrate. 'She was so elegant.'

'She was, yes.' My mother was at her side, rubbing her back.

'Do you remember the cream trouser suit that she used to wear with the black polo-neck?' Her voice was plaintive. 'Do you, Johanna?'

'She does this,' my father said across to me. 'Sharp as a tack one minute and then talking nonsense. The cancer's in her brain now.'

'She's not deaf, Dad.'

'Don't attack your father,' my mother scolded. 'He's right.'

'I'm writing a film about her, Beth,' my

grandmother said. 'About Mummy. I'd like to get Sophia Loren to play the leading role. I've written to her. Did I tell you that?'

'No, you didn't tell me.'

'And,' she crossed her bony fingers and waved them as she spoke, 'she hasn't said no.'

'I think she'd be perfect.'

'Yes! Wouldn't she? That's what I said. She has her colouring. And her spirit! I try to tell your mother here about it but she just laughs at me. She thinks I'm mad.'

I smiled.

'But what would she know? She thinks you're mad too.'

★ ★ ★

Agnes died the following Monday. For two days, her body lay in state in the front sitting room — the 'good room' — in my parents' house, staring up at the chandelier she'd bought them as a wedding gift. I stood in the hall outside the door.

I wanted to preserve Agnes and the room as they were, to know them only the way they had always been.

Her fierce and proud, fond of saying, 'It'll all come out in the wash,' and nodding her head.

The good room static with the rose-print

tea set I'd always been forbidden to touch sitting ready on the sideboard for some event that would never happen; the unused silver-service cutlery in the open felt-lined drawer; the Oriental rug bought in town when I was a child and my father had started to make what he called 'real' money.

And now there was a corpse. In the good room.

I didn't go in.

★ ★ ★

The priest spoke with a drone and left long pauses between his sentences. Agnes would have told him to get a move on. My mother kept her composure, but her face was pale and its lines deeper. She did the first reading and her voice was thin and fragile so it didn't carry.

'She gave out big breaths, maybe five or six of them, before her body just *deflated*. Within minutes, she looked almost entirely flat,' she told me, as we left the church. 'So papery and so harmless, in the end.'

During the service at the cemetery, she stood linking my arm. I felt her squeeze it against her side when the coffin was being blessed. I moved to put it around her and caught her panicked expression. I followed her eyes and saw what it was that had upset her: standing among the mourners, behind my father, was Gloria, the bridge player with the wild hair.

Once the prayers had finished, Gloria was next to him, leaning in for an embrace. My father put his hands on her upper arms to control the gesture.

'Why would he give that woman an ounce of his time?' My mother was frantic as I walked her to the mourning car. 'I don't understand it. She has no decorum *and* she smokes. Your father gave up smoking twenty years ago. He can do anything once he sets his mind to it. He has marvellous willpower, your father.'

The first car left with my mother and her brothers in it. My father announced that he would drive himself and the outgoing captain of the golf club to the hotel. A ruddy-faced man wearing the Woodford blazer said nothing but shook my hand and patted my shoulder.

As his car was reversing out of its space, I saw Gloria approach my father's window and give it a little tap with her nail. The window went down and she spoke into it for a moment — from where I was standing I could see that her back was hollowed, one leg bent and raised off the ground, her ankle making coquettish circles. Then she opened the door behind him and got in. As the car pulled away, I saw her lean forward between the two men in the front seats, tilt her head toward my father and say something. She was laughing when she waved at me as they passed.

If It Weren't for the Weather

The day got off to a tepid start when I woke and remembered that Saoirse's Christmas Gathering was that evening. It had been scheduled for this weekend to coincide with the completion of something she called the 'drawing room'.

The first snow of the winter had fallen the previous night and the reflected light glared into our bedroom as I drew back the curtains. White car-shapes were parked in driveways and snow had gathered in little banks at the front doors opposite. Robert, dressed head-to-toe in royal-blue ski gear, was already out in his garden spraying anti-freeze into the car locks. Anna, wearing a chalky-pink adult-babygro affair with zippers in every direction, was monitoring his progress.

★ ★ ★

Saoirse opened her door in a complicated ensemble of cream sheaths and gauzy fabrics that had no beginning or end.

'Bloody snow,' she said, kissing the air on both sides of me while frantically moving her

243

leg to dry our footprints with a cream towel under her shoe. 'The parquet flooring wasn't built for it.'

She kissed air near Steve and near Al. And then she bent down to Mae's level.

'How do you do, Ismae?' she said clearly and loudly, extending a hand as though one of them were the queen.

'Hello,' said Mae, taking off her hat and lying it on Saoirse's outstretched palm.

★ ★ ★

An impressive log fire dominated the sitting room, two beautifully decorated Christmas trees flanking it, one on each side. Delicate orchids in fluted vases looked shy next to giant platters of truffles in complex pyramid formations. I didn't dare disturb their arrangement by eating one. Saoirse's husband, Peter, was busy art-directing their six-year-old son Felim around the house and filming his anxious moves.

'If you must play with your friends or run to the door when the bell rings, at least look back at Daddy and smile or laugh when you're doing it,' Peter was saying. 'Whatever feels natural, son.'

I'd never seen Peter dressed casually before and his voice seemed peculiar without a three-piece suit.

'Oh, hello there, Beth. Steve.' He nodded at us. 'And a Happy Christmas to you both. Say hello to Alex and Ismae, Felim. Just a second — hang on. OK: now.'

Neighbours stood around the walls exchanging views about trivial things. Nobody sat down yet, afraid to commit to a chair and get stuck with the wrong person.

Anna and Moirah stood together by the fire, two fantasy witches conspiring. 'Well, what can you expect from them?' Moirah was saying. 'They watch television eating their breakfast!' and she released a loud, joyless laugh into the air. I set my drink down on the closed piano.

'What an amusing little gift,' Saoirse was saying out in the hallway. She came into the room, something small held out from her body between her thumb and forefinger. When she set it down on the sideboard, I saw it was a marble Buddha.

'I mean, honestly,' she said to me, in a quietly exasperated voice. 'Where am I supposed to put *that*? In *this* house.' And then, 'But you might like to have it?'

'Is Sommer here?' I asked.

'Sommer?' She tilted her head and frowned. 'Do you know I never even thought to ask her. She'd most likely have said no, anyway. I don't think we're her kind of people.'

'That's true,' I said.

From where I was standing by Saoirse's bay window, I could see the edge of the lintel supporting our front door. I remembered the first day Steve and I went through that door, to view the house. The top lock slipped on it when we were inside so when we had finished marvelling at the number of rooms, all the spaces, our imagined list of practicalities, we found we couldn't leave unless we opened one of the front windows downstairs and climbed out into the driveway. The house wanted to keep us, we'd agreed. At the time, we saw this as a good thing.

Before then, I'd never thought I'd live somewhere like this; not happily anyway. And I'd been right. I hadn't been happy. I felt like a nomad in a settled camp.

'Lovely. That looks great,' Peter's voice complimenting his son's smiles competed with the Three Tenors CD. Saoirse stood watching her husband for a moment, her face full of admiration as though he was furniture she had chosen, a dresser that was appreciating with age.

I noticed that the men at the party fell broadly into two categories: those who talked too much and those who said nothing at all. I was surprised to see that Jack Moore was there, a man who spent most of the year travelling and writing about his experiences for a Sunday broadsheet. 'Unusual' and 'peculiar' were words his neighbours were most likely to use about him.

'I'm just back from Borneo, actually,' he was saying to Kate.

'How interesting,' she said. And then, 'I like your shirt,' she remarked almost immediately, bringing the conversation onto more manageable ground.

I picked up my glass; only a lemon wedge sat in the end of it so I put it back down again.

Anna handed Steve a glass of red wine and made a place for herself standing between us. Steve turned and handed me the glass. 'You have it, Bethy. Yours is empty. I'll go and see what Mae is up to.'

'Beth — do come and see my new *drawing room*. Let me show you it. You can bring him too, if you like.' Saoirse's eyes were half-closed as she spoke grandly and motioned at Al who was next to me. 'Once he has no food or drink with him.'

Al gave a little mock bow. *Why thank you, kind lady.*

We followed her down the hallway in silence.

She leaned heavily on the door that led to a space formerly known as the back room.

'I think you'll get quite a surprise,' she said in a hushed tone.

The door opened slowly, scraping over thick, white carpet. Inside, the air in the room was fibrous and muggy. We were breaking the seal on a sacred tomb. The carpet had straight lines made by the vacuum cleaner running along it, just like the ones from the mower on her front lawn. Blinding white walls bounced light off an antique gold chandelier that hung from the middle of a centre rose. White, panelled shelves were bare except for the occasional futile but perfectly placed thing: a slender vase of elegant fake ferns, the tiniest ceramic bowl I'd ever seen, a single crystal candlestick, and other objects of that nature.

And then I saw it: a gilt-edged painted portrait of Saoirse, Peter and Felim staring maniacally into the room hung above the marble fireplace. Saoirse and Peter were sitting on throne-like chairs, Felim standing between them, his hand on his mother's knee. It may just have been the fright I got, but it looked as though they were actually life-sized. I wanted to laugh aloud.

'Do you love it, Beth?' she asked me. 'You can absolutely say if you don't,' she lied.

'I absolutely do,' I said, only noticing I had mimicked her when it was too late.

'The room or the portrait?' she pressed.

'Both,' I said, because we all have our little pretences, the things we agree with in order to survive.

'Reeeeeaalllly?' She spread the word up and down and out.

I looked at Al. His eyes were wide, fixed on the painting.

'It's very impressive,' he said. 'Everyone here will love it.' He already understood the dance of the suburbs.

'Mama. Wee wee.' Mae was in the hall looking for me. 'Mama! Go wee wee!'

'Oh, goodness. Quick, you better get to her,' said Saoirse, ushering us out of the tomb and toward the under-stairs bathroom. 'Oh! There's someone in there! I suppose you'd better take her straight up to the bathroom at the top of the stairs. Don't mind the mess. Go — quickly!'

The upstairs of Saoirse's showhouse, where nobody went, comprised the same grid of boxy rooms as my own, but these boxes were wildly unkempt and connected by a trail of dishevelled clothes, books, and bits of toys that lay strewn across the floor.

'F to the A to the I to the L,' Al said behind me as the three of us picked our way through dirty socks and old newspaper supplements.

When we came back downstairs, I saw Steve was trapped talking to Noel who lived

249

three doors away from us. Noel liked to upgrade his conversation by mentioning a celebrity or someone he considered noteworthy every couple of sentences. I noticed that when it was Steve's turn to speak, Noel's lips kept moving silently, as though rehearsing his next line, so I thought he couldn't really be listening.

And then Saoirse was at my side, speaking unusually gently.

'It's hard to keep everything 'just so' all the time, isn't it?' she said quietly, and motioned toward her upstairs.

'It really is,' I said. 'Sometimes when Steve comes in, he thinks we've been burgled with the mess in the house!' I smiled at her. 'And look at the beautiful job you've done down here.'

She gave my arm a little squeeze. And I kind of liked her.

Then she bellowed, 'IT'S TIME FOR NIBBLES!' into the room. 'Everybody! Come along. Just little bits and pieces, you know; but they're all Fairtrade. Well, the ham is. Or it's organic anyway. And the other things are certainly *ethical,* I'm assured. Peter will do the carving, won't you, darling? And then everyone can dig in themselves. Peter? PETER! Oh, there you are. Can you see to the ham? Please.'

'Can ham be unfairly traded?' Jack Moore

250

asked into the air. 'I suppose it can.'

'And there are lots of other bits. Just help yourselves. No frilly cake here, Anna!' She laughed and nodded at Anna, who took her cue and joined in the laughter.

'I saw Janine Woods, you know from the school,' Anna started into the tale, 'picking up a cake yesterday at the baker's in the village. And it had *piping* around it. Frilly, piped icing! On a Christmas cake. She must have been late for a carvery dinner in the seventies!'

I couldn't talk myself into parties like this any longer. I couldn't live in rooms like this anymore. I felt like a child trapped in a car seat on an interminably long journey. Going nowhere. I looked around for Steve, needing to see him, to see the kids, to get some air. He and Al were kneeling on the floor at the glass doors to the garden, Mae standing between them, all three ignoring the nonsense talk of ethical ham and embarrassing cake. He and Al were each drawing a heart in breathy condensation on the glass.

'For Mae,' Al said of his and wrote her name above it.

'For Al,' Steve said and wrote the name above his.

And then Mae reached her chubby hand out and drew a big, wobbly heart on the sweated window with her index finger.

'For Mama,' she said and Steve held her finger while she made an 'M' inside it. 'And Dada,' she said then, and they made a 'D' inside it too.

I went to Mae and touched her cheek to steady myself; she was my smooth little worry stone.

* * *

'You're sure you won't stay?' Saoirse asked as we left.

'No, it's getting a little late for us. But thank you.'

Steve and Al each took one of Mae's hands and swung her down the driveway and out onto the street.

'Of course. Hopefully things will wind up here soon anyway; we're having our family photo taken for the front of this year's Christmas card tomorrow.'

'Oh. Lovely.'

'Did you want me to see if the photographer has time to pop over to yours after he's finished here? He's terribly good.'

'Thanks, but no. I don't think we'll bother with that; we don't usually.' I turned and started down her driveway. 'Good night now.'

'Is it because of Mae?' she called from the door.

'Pardon?' I stopped and half-turned back around.

'Is it because of Mae?' Saoirse repeated, taking a couple of steps toward me and dropping her voice. 'That you don't do a portrait Christmas card. Because I just want you to know, Beth, that I understand. I mean, I know you don't think it but I hate a lot of this stuff too. All the — *keeping up*. Anyway, I completely see why you wouldn't want to be sending out a card with a family photo on the front when Mae — '

'No.' I couldn't bear to hear her finish the sentence. 'It is not because of my beautiful daughter.' My temper was rising into my throat but I held it. Saoirse had her struggles too. 'Enjoy the rest of your evening and thanks again for having us.'

Up ahead, I could see Al pretending to chase Mae, running in slow motion, while she squealed and giggled so much that she started to hiccough.

I caught up with Steve and linked his arm. He kissed me on the forehead, snowflakes swirling down around us.

'I've been thinking,' I said.

'Hmmm?'

'That we really need to get the fuck out of here.'

Land of the Long White Cloud

'How come this plane already smells of coffee and stale peanuts?' Al asks into my ear. While he's leaning into me, the seat in front of him jerks backwards so his table-top is almost rubbing his lap. He does a double take.

'Seriously?' His face is full of horror. 'We're *still on the ground.*'

He starts to untangle the lead from his earphones. 'I bet he waits until the stewardess parks her drinks trolley in the aisle to *need* to squeeze out urgently to the toilet. And she'll have to reverse twelve rows to accommodate him. Then he'll barrel down to the toilet and wait in a queue with five other fools all standing looking at their empty seats. I can't bear people on planes.' He puts his iPod earphones in and closes his eyes. 'Wake me when we get there.'

Beside him, Mae is standing on her seat, her little head brushing off the reading light in the panel. Steve is folding his legs up to his chest to fit into his seat from the aisle.

I lean against the window and try not to think about how much I hate flying. The Perspex moves a little in its casing with the weight of my head. I sit up straight and look around. Across the aisle from Steve a lady with her neck encased in a plastic horseshoe-shaped pillow sits stiffly so as not to disturb it.

I think about our decision to make this trip. It was made on the day after Saoirse's party when I came home from having my opinions corrected by my mother and found Mae and Steve painting pictures at the kitchen table. Mae had lifted her page to show me as soon as I walked in. She had painted a face, as she always liked to. She'd clambered down from her seat, taking care not to smudge her painting and stuck it up on the fridge with a magnet. Then she stood back to admire it. 'Nice,' she said, smiling.

'Very nice, Mae. A face.'

'*My* face,' she clarified.

'Good. Your face. Beautiful.'

Steve had stayed at the table finishing his. His face was serious, intent on his creation, using Mae's six little pots of paint and three withered brushes. He was biting down on his bottom lip when he eventually turned his around for me to see. It was the inside of a boat sailing toward a harbour. Four pairs of shoes in different sizes were sitting on the deck. Our sail-boat dream of twenty years ago. That afternoon, we booked the tickets to spend a few weeks to see how it would be.

The captain announces we have landed in Auckland, where the temperature outside is 26 degrees and the local time is 1.35 p.m.

We all stand up too soon, open overhead bins, gather bags and jackets and scarves and rubbish and crouch half-bent in the space of our seats. Then, after an age, we get going, as far as the aisle, and stand with our overloaded arms, breathing each others impatience for another forever.

But then, we get out.

Steve pushes our tower of bags through the doors of the airport and stops on the pavement. He squeezes my hand before letting it go and walking to the edge of the kerb. He splays his arms, palms up, and, as he feels the familiar warmth, he seems to me to get broader, his neck to get longer, The sunny glare bounces up from the tarmac and onto the bonnet of a white taxi pulling in.

Mae runs to him and hugs his leg.

He turns and looks at me.

'I can feel it. Can you? Can you feel the difference?'

And I can. Freedom and warmth. I nod.

★ ★ ★

Mae plays with a little shell on the sand and I watch the others — my son, my husband, and his father — as the motor catches and the little boat moves away from us across the bay.

Later, I watch them as they gut the fish they've caught and place them on the barbecue. I notice Al's easy laughter. Here, I don't have to draw him out with tea and snacks and control of the television remote. Here, he is unfurled, his face flooded with life. Animated, amphibious. His father is enjoying things himself — the view, the sun, the water — as if he is seeing them for the first time in years too. Steve comes over and stoops down to where I sit, both our faces underneath the brim of my hat. He kisses me slowly, twice, there in our little shade. His father smiles over, unembarrassed by this tenderness.

Later we walk to the top of the volcanic Mount Eden with its twisted Pohutukawa trees smothering in their own bright scarlet flowers; sunbursts in January. Mae's fourth birthday is next week and it will be her first in the sunshine.

★   ★   ★

Steve meets his two closest friends and all three pick up the friendship like it's a bag on the ground between their feet. I stop what I'm doing and watch them and already I understand him better. We go to dinner at the harbour with their families. They ask me what I do for fun at home and I can't think of anything so I say that I read. Al says he has always been interested in art and drawing and they love that. Then he says that he really enjoyed driving the boat and spearing fish in the bay yesterday. And they love that too. Mae says that she likes to 'dance!' and gets down onto the boardwalk in her bare feet to show them her little scuttling crab moves.

I look up at the sky and wish upon an inky star.

★ ★ ★

It's the seventeenth of January and Mae is four today.

It's the day on the calendar that I dread every year since 2010. It's the day when I must not only dwell on, but *celebrate*, the worst event of my life.

I watch her play and I think how in the past I've wondered if Down syndrome is the world's most perfect payback for the selfish or errant woman. The pain is the mother's. The child is happy, loved, and largely unaware of — and therefore untouched by — her disability, by how some people stare while others can't bring themselves to look at all.

But this year the pain is less. I watch her confidently climbing the steps and then coming down the slide, over and over again. Up and down, up and down in her little yellow sunhat. And every time she gets to the bottom she punches the air with both fists, her victorious arms stretched up straight into the blue sky. She loves her life. And I feel I have won even though I don't deserve to.

Al is lying on the grass with his pencils and sketch book. He is drawing Mae to record this unusual year — her birthday in the sun.

Steve and I are sitting at the harbour-side watching our children. Being next to the water is loosening something in each of us. I look over beyond the lushness of Mount Victoria and the view is enormous. And I realise that he is right. It is a different kind of green.

★   ★   ★

On our last day, Steve goes to mass with his father. I hear the jeep coming back, the noise of loose metal on the gravelly path. I watch Steve's father struggle to get down from his seat. His brown legs have become thin over the last few years.

When the time comes for us to leave, his father looks down and picks at a button on his shirt. He's eighty-five now.

Mae admires her sun-pink face in the wing mirror of the car and says, 'Mama — stay? Please?' while Steve puts our cases into the boot.

On the way to the airport, the four of us stop off at the Waitomo Caves to see the grotto of glow-worms. We go through the caves in a canoe, the worms hanging down like fairy lights — tiny ideas in the darkness. Al and Mae love it, the magical worms and their life of instinct upside-down.

How easily I could leave what I know, my life the right way up. I could step out of it like it was a skin I'd shed because I no longer have any use for it. I am small and free and separate from things here, and I like it. I have nobody to run to when things go wrong, nobody to consult, nobody to pacify. And I like that too. I feel excited by the possibility that maybe I'm nicer here than at home. Friendlier. Less serious. Able to breathe.

In this little canoe in the dark, I can feel myself at the door to a different way of being, a different place where Steve could be the leader. I am giddy to let him push it open.

We are all quiet when we get back into the car homeward bound.

The Foolish Path

My mother was kneeling on a small, rectangular mat wearing green leather gardening gloves with a lavender turn-up. She lifted her head as my car parked in front of her. Her face was fully made up.

'Hello there,' she shouted loudly and waved her arm, as though beckoning a distant boat. She was being over-buoyant, so I knew there was something wrong.

'Hi, Mum.'

'My darlings! Lovely!' she bellowed as she stood up and started to remove her gloves.

'You should really think about wearing a hat when you're out in the sun.'

'Beth, you know it doesn't agree with my hair to wear a hat. That's an interesting dress, darling. You look very *current*.'

'Where's Dad?'

'Granny, you should really get a hat for when you're in the garden.' Al came from behind the car, having found his basketball in the boot. 'The sun was shining right on the top of your head there.'

'Oh, Alex. You are kind to think of me. I should have a hat but no matter how many hints I drop, nobody seems to want to buy me one!'

I shook my head at her so he would see.

'Let's all go inside and I'll be ready to leave with you in a jiffy' she said. 'I hope you didn't mind picking me up?'

'Of course not. There's no point in you and Dad having two cars up at our house. Where is he?'

'He said he'd be along in half an hour.' Her hand went up to her earring. 'I hope the lunch won't spoil, waiting for him?'

'Where is he?'

'I heard you the first time, Beth.' Her voice was irritated. 'I don't know where he is. He didn't say.'

Driving to Vesey Hill, we passed a man wearing a tracksuit leaning against a wall licking an ice-cream cone. My mother checked the lock on her passenger door with her elbow.

★   ★   ★

'So . . . We're planning a move to New Zealand.' I clumsily threw it into the air. 'You know how it's always been on the cards. Well — '

'What?' My mother made a big show of steadying herself by grabbing hold of the back of a chair.

'We've decided to move, Mum. To New Zealand. At the end of the year.'

'This year? Have you gone out of your mind?'

'No.' I smiled. 'I know it's a lot to take in but we think now is the right time. We've been planning it for months.'

Steve and Al had gone to pick up some dessert so that I could tell her by myself. But I knew they wouldn't be long and I could see she was gathering her thoughts. Her words wouldn't be far behind them, so I pushed on while I had the chance.

'It's always been a possibility. I mean, you know that Steve has been keen for us to make a life out there for, well, for years really . . . '

She sighed as though trying to humour a delusional maniac. And then she spoke slowly. 'In normal circumstances, Beth, this might be seen as something exciting, as an opportunity. But your circumstances are hardly normal now, are, they?'

And then she was off, gaining speed as she went. 'You will simply never manage. You have a *Down syndrome child*. I'm as open to thinking outside the square as the next person, everyone knows that about me, but this strikes me as foolishness. In fact — I can tell you that it won't work.' Her voice was gathering grit. 'I *know* you, Beth. It will never work. You need support. *And* you like your routine; it's what makes you happy.'

She couldn't have been more wrong.

'You don't value things, value what you have. And, clearly, neither does Steve.'

'We do. It may just be that we have a different set of values to you.'

'You simply won't manage.'

'Maybe I'll surprise you.'

'I very much doubt it.' She gave a little snort. 'I mean, what will you *do* all the way over there?'

'I expect I'll start writing again.'

She rolled her eyes.

'Well, I don't. I expect you will be all over the place and not get a minute for yourself, with no supports. It'll be like here; you won't write a word.'

'Well, luckily, 'not writing' is something I can do from anywhere.'

She continued talking, no time now for listening. 'The children will suffer. I think what you're suggesting is very reckless. And, what's more, it's selfish, Beth, I have to say.'

'The children will not suffer. The schools are very good and the climate will certainly be much better for Mae, for a start.'

In my imaginings, Mae's coughs and colds would dry up and her body would uncurl and grow toward the clear sky.

'Climate! For goodness sake. Young people and their obsession with good weather. Honestly. There's more to life than blasted sunshine, Beth.' She motioned at the window. 'Anyway, it's sunny here.'

'Today. It's the second mild day this year and it's almost June.'

'I've heard it rains a lot more there than you would think.'

I sighed and she turned away. Silence filled the kitchen. She picked up a cloth and started wiping at my clean worktop.

'This just isn't what we want, Mum. It doesn't seem like the right way to live. For us.'

'What does that even *mean*?' Her voice was loud as she spun around and looked me right in the eyes.

'Mum, Mae is upstairs,' I said as I shut the door.

'Well?'

'I hate this estate, if you must know. I actually hate living here. It's a horrible aspirational place.'

'Since when?'

'Since bloody always. And I'm sick of hanging around here waiting for our lives to begin. For something to happen.'

'I don't even know what you're talking about now. It just seems like you're doing this to — to get my attention. Why must you insist on pulling out of me, Beth? Looking for me to support you in ways you know that I can't. It's always been like this. Demanding things of me that I can't give.'

Her chest was covered in red blotches now.

'We will go, Mum. It's the right thing for us.'

She set her mouth in a line.

'Plenty of women would give their right arm to have what you have here.' She waved her own right arm around the room. 'This lovely house, such pleasant neighbours.'

'Most of them are vile, Mum. And anyway, I don't want to be born and live and die in the one postcode. There are other places, other opportunities, other experiences for us, for Mae, and for Al.'

'Oh, yes — poor Alex. What does he think? He has lots of lovely friends that he couldn't possibly want to leave.'

I laughed. She stiffened and put her hand over her purse whenever one of these 'lovely' teenagers came into the house.

'He's happy to go. To see more of the world. He knows we will come back if he doesn't settle.'

'I don't even know why I'm trying to make you see sense, Beth. Why I'm trying to talk you out of it. I mean, there's probably quite a positive side to you not calling in on top of your father and me all the time. All of us in each other's hair.'

'Thanks.'

'Oh, you know what I'm saying!'

And I did. She would be more able to cocoon him, to better keep him for herself without us as a disturbance, visiting and taking his attention.

'Anyway. None of this matters.' Her voice was defiant. 'None of this matters because your father will never agree to it.'

'He doesn't have to. He's not invited.'

★ ★ ★

Almost an hour later, the might of my father came marching through the door before Steve had a chance to open it fully.

'There you are, Steve.'

'There *you* are, Dermot.'

'I kept your lunch for you but it might be past its best at this stage,' I said, as he came into the kitchen.

'I'm not hungry. I've just had lunch. That's why I'm late.'

'Oh.'

He looked at my mother at the table. 'With John from the club,' he added.

'Is there coffee?' he asked, his palms

upwards, eyes wide. He didn't tend to bother with tea. It didn't have enough to offer him.

My mother jumped up and set about filling the kettle.

'Beth and Steve have news, darling,' she said while her back was to us all.

'Oh, yes?' My father looked at me.

'We're thinking of moving to New Zealand.' I spoke quickly, pushed into the centre of the circle at a kids' party.

'Actually, Dermot, we're more than thinking about it. We have made the decision to go.' My husband said what I couldn't. 'We've been planning it since February.'

'I did try to talk sense to your daughter, Dermot. But she won't listen.' Her tone was brittle now with my father's back up. 'Apparently she hates this estate and everyone in it.'

Steve smiled at me when he heard her say this. He looked like he might laugh.

My father ignored her.

'It's like you must forever take a different path, a path that I have no understanding of,' she went on, pitching herself against me.

'What will you do out there?' My father spoke.

'I asked that already and couldn't get a straight answer.' She was triumphant.

'For money. What will you do, Steven? It

doesn't grow on trees, you know.'

'I know that, Dermot.' Steve smiled. 'I'll be working in the same area, much as I do now here and in London. But actually with better terms. A lot less travel. I have meetings already set up.'

My father raised mean eyebrows. 'And will any of them come to anything? I mean, by *meetings* I hope you don't mean going for a beer with chaps you knew when you lived there in the nineties.' He laughed, but nothing about it was funny. 'You're a bit late in life to be starting up, expecting things to work themselves out.'

'I'm not starting up, Dermot, and age is one of the reasons Beth and I want to do this now. Before the children — well, Al, really — get too old and aren't happy to go. I have few convictions about things these days, but I believe this will be a good move for all of us. We'll be leaving before the end of the year. We'll be in New Zealand for the summer. Their summer.'

My mother gave an audible sigh. 'Not the infernal sun again.'

'We should have gone years ago, Dad. If I hadn't felt so paralysed after Mae was born, we'd have had the courage to go. It's taken me this long to feel confident, ready — more than ready. We need to go now; I need to go.'

My father put his hand on my shoulder and a moment passed before he turned to Steve.

'A plan is the thing, Steven. You don't want to be working long hours when you should be enjoying your pension. I've always measured out my time, planned well ahead, Steven.' I hadn't heard him call him Steven in over a decade. Three times now in a couple of minutes. 'That's why I am where I am today.'

My husband didn't want to measure out his time, didn't want to be where my father was today, ever, but he said nothing.

'I've tried to plan my life, Dad, and it's never got me anywhere. So now, this.' It was my turn to make a statement. 'This is it.'

'The smart thing to do in life is to protect yourself, protect your freedom. You know, batten down the hatches, take root. Gather in your supports. This seems as though you are taking on a lot. Pulling up your roots. Is that what you want?'

'Yes, Dad. I think it is.'

'Where will you stay when you visit?' my mother suddenly squawked. 'We couldn't accommodate all of you in our house! So you'd have to keep a place here. Or make arrangements to stay somewhere else. We just don't have the room, not at our age.'

My father squeezed his eyes tightly shut and pinched the bridge of his nose.

'You've upset your father now, Beth.' My mother's voice was quiet.

'Will you please just make that coffee!' he snapped over his shoulder at her.

After a silence, he opened his eyes and spoke to no one and everyone. 'I will miss the children. Very much. I don't want to dwell on it.'

He stood and crossed the floor to the bay window. The four gold buttons on his Woodford blazer shone.

'That's a fine-looking car over there. Whose is that?' he asked.

I noticed his bulk could take most of the light from the room.

'It's Robert's,' I said. 'You know, the guy with the oiled hair. The one you think has a toupee.'

'Very impressive. What does he do?'

'Oh, for heaven's sake!' My mother was furious at the sudden lack of crisis. An opportunity for her and my father to bond through distress was being wasted. She put the coffee pot and a cup down next to him and then linked her arm through his.

'Who cares about Robert or his silly car!' Her voice quietened as she addressed my father with a coo. 'Darling, don't you think they have such a, such a *comfortable* life here? I mean, they're settled here.' Her lipstick had faded to a thin red outline around her mouth.

'Well, clearly they aren't bloody *settled,* Johanna. If they were, they'd hardly be leaving, would they?' and he walked out of the room leaving everything said.

★   ★   ★

I tried to focus on the good things to come over the next six months, our last ones here. But even with the romance of knowing we were leaving, I struggled. Instead, I thought about the Waitomo glow-worms and the shine from their upside-down world.

Just Like That

At first, I thought the evening might go well.

It was dark as we came into Woodford Golf Club and the lights from the dining room shone outside. Snow had fallen this November morning and the floor-to-ceiling glass showed the covered greens, the trees heaving with the early winter weight, quietly melting white.

I watched my daughter as she politely observed the room from the doorway. She was wearing the polka-dot dress with the net underskirt and furry stole that my mother had bought her especially for this party. A hideous ensemble — I'd considered changing her just before we left the house but thought, *It's the Last Time. It's the Last Time.*

Mae was nearly five now and, underskirt and stole aside, she looked beautiful. The worried kind of love I'd thought I would always feel for her was fading away as she grew and learned and played and spoke, and in its place a calm adoration was laying itself down.

'Really, Beth. Must Alex wear his hair like that when he's coming here?'

My mother had appeared from the bowels of the room and was loud-whispering into my ear. She half-hugged me with one arm, holding her glass of wine out at arm's length.

I stroked the crown of Mae's head to comfort myself.

'It's a form of expression.'

'I see. And exactly what is it he's trying to say?'

I refused her question by looking away.

'And to think I was worried about *my* hairstyle,' she went on. 'I had to go to that girl in the village to have my blow dry this morning. I don't like going there — I find her a *bit much*, to be honest — but with everything that's been going on I totally forgot about myself and making an appointment in town.'

My mother's hair was in exactly the same sculpted formations as always.

I looked at the beige wall of old framed photos of men behind her. Old frames, old photos, and old men.

'The most interesting people in this club are all dead.' I heard my father's voice approaching us. He had noticed me looking at the Woodford wall of fame. 'With the exception of myself, of course.' He put his arm around my shoulders. 'Hi, Bethy. And my gorgeous princess.' He hunched down

274

and pressed his nose against Mae's. Then she climbed onto his back. He straightened himself with the appearance of ease, like always, as Mae beamed over his shoulder.

'Hi, Big Man.' He shook Al's hand. 'I like your hair like that.'

'Thanks, Grandad.'

My mother tutted and took herself off to see to something or other.

'Steve, why don't you and Al get stuck into some of those fancy little food things that are all over the place down there.' He motioned further into the room. The women in the burgundy waistcoats were on their toes this evening — dickie bows straight, trays aloft.

Steve nodded at him and kissed my cheek.

And then it was just us on the edge of a room by a window — my dad holding my daughter, and me.

'Well, here we are. A going-away party. You can still change your mind, though, you know.' He smiled at me. 'We could just run for it, you and I. And Daisy Mae here.'

I smiled back. 'No. I'm good. But thanks.'

'I'm game if you are.'

'I think I'm going to stick with this one, Dad.'

'You're sure it's what you want?'

I could hear that he was asking me a real question, a bigger question, and that the situation called for a clear and honest answer.

'Yes, I'm absolutely sure.'

'Well, then. If it's good enough for you, it's good enough for me.'

I motioned at the window. 'The course looks beautiful.'

'Yes, thank you,' he said. Somehow taking credit for snow.

★ ★ ★

A flare from my single days, Jilly had come and, according to my mother, already drunk an amount of wine that was 'far in excess of good manners, whether it's free or not'.

'WHAT'S YOUR NAME?' Jilly spoke loudly and slowly to Mae.

Turning to me before Mae had a chance to reply, she said, 'She's so precious — is she verbal?'

'I'm Mae. Hello,' my daughter answered.

'OH! HELLO. How lovely. I don't have any children, Beth. My husband, Colm — I don't think you've ever met him, no, you wouldn't have — well, anyway, he never wanted any. Said they were too costly.' She bent down to Mae's level. 'WHAT DO YOU THINK OF THAT, MAE?'

Mae shrugged and looked at me. I shrugged back.

'YOU'RE LUCKY, MAE,' Jilly said. 'YOU'LL NEVER GET MARRIED.'

*   *   *

Because he was at a table full of men — the kind of men who wore ties at the weekend — my father's voice had become loud. He talked and talked, pausing only to have another of the chocolates on the table before tossing the scrunched-up wrapper back into the bowl. I caught parts of his conversation.

'I don't suffer fools. Ask anybody and they'll tell you that Dermot O'Connor doesn't suffer fools.'

Every so often he laughed like a foghorn until the others joined in. His talk was primarily about people: lady golfers ('Some of them are doing alright but sure they've no drive') and artists ('Expecting the rest of us to fund their grants so they can *find themselves*') and women who hyphenate their surnames ('Feminists. More annoying than the bloody artists.') Then he moved on to what's wrong with the world ('Laziness. And artists') and what the world needs more of ('Loyalty. And hard workers').

I laughed despite myself. And I thought of how strong he could be and how certain of his own ideas. And I felt a pain I hadn't expected as I wondered if I'd miss how he spoke, how definite he could sound, how sure he had been for me when I'd really needed him to be.

The waiter brought his Scotch and set it in front of him on a circular mat. My father didn't say anything to him, nor even acknowledge him with a gesture.

And I thought I might just be OK.

★ ★ ★

The stressed-out actress who resembled my mother was laughing inanely, part of a group of women in their seventies who were well acquainted, but not friendly, with each other.

'Your top is lovely, Annabel. Gorgeous.'

'This thing? Oh, thank you.'

'That grey really suits you.'

'Yes, it goes with my hair!'

Altogether now — Ha ha ha.

My mother turned to me as I passed behind her. 'I'm not feeling the best, darling. I'm going to step outside for some air.'

I followed her out onto the terrace. It had been decorated with fairy lights along the railings, and there were two outside heaters.

'Are you OK, Mum?'

The self-closing door successfully slammed itself behind me.

'Christ! Those doors! They'd have your head off. Your father warned them before they had them put in but they couldn't be told. They should have listened to him.'

'Mum, is something the matter? It's about two degrees out here.'

'I'm just a bit *out of kilter*. While I was fixing my face in the mirror before we came out, your father *announced* that he has always — always! — thought that the amount of make-up a woman uses is proportional to her self-confidence. The more confident she is, the less make-up she wears, he said.'

My mother wore a lot of make-up.

'Then he slapped the light off and walked out of the room, the way he does, leaving me in semi-darkness!'

'He's always doing that. He has a thing about preserving power.'

'It doesn't stop him going out when it's freezing cold and leaving the door wide open. He'd let me perish.'

Two blobs of mascara sat on her cheek, having fallen from her stiff, over-black lashes. I took a tissue from my bag and brushed them away. She looked exhausted, the skin around her eyes crêpey and dark.

'What was it?' she asked, looking at my hand.

'Just a bit of dust or something. Nothing.'

She nodded. 'Honestly, Beth. I can't keep it up. There's no more terrifying thing than feeling that your relationship, your home life, everything, might be under threat. Sometimes, really, I don't even know who it is I am.'

'I can understand that, Mum.'

'Of course you can.' She took my hand. 'I forget you've been through so much, darling. You're strong, you see. Like your father. You're copers, both of you. I'm not sure that I am.'

'Oh, Mum. You've done OK. All these years being married to Dad. He might be strong but he's no picnic.'

'Can I tell you something?' She looked up at me with a weary face. 'You mightn't like it. But now that it seems you might actually go through with this *move* . . . ' She lengthened the word to make nonsense of it.

'Of course.' I ignored the inference and sat down on the bench beside her, into the orangey glow from the heater.

'In the early months, after little Ismae was born — you remember that time, everything was so all over the place — well, for a while — I used to wonder which of us got the worse deal: me with my baby dying, you know, my boy, or you having your little baby with Down syndrome. I hope you don't mind me saying this now, but I have to get it off my chest.' She blinked her eyes to stop the tears in their blackened tracks.

'What a horrible thing for me to think. You must hate me for it. To have thought it would be better if Ismae hadn't . . . I'm sorry but it was different in my day, different for those children.' I could hear something raw and *real* in her voice. 'The . . . acceptance, the way people . . . it wasn't like now.'

My mother and I had lived in some kind of opposition to each other for as long as I could remember but here in the cold she was volunteering something honest and warm. She could do it because we both knew it wouldn't have to be maintained for long. We had only days left.

I put one arm around her shoulder.

'I understand, Mum. I really do, because, do you know what? I thought it too. Her own mother. I wondered if I'd have preferred her to be taken from me rather than have to fight and speak for her all my life.' I was quiet for a minute. 'And then, after a longer time than I'm proud of, I moved on from that and I fell in love with her. But then, then that fear I'd felt around her changed into something even worse.' I stopped, readying myself to say something I'd never said aloud before. 'I thought that she would . . . go, you know

. . . that she'd die, that she'd *have* to die, to redress the balance for what I did years ago. When I was a teenager.'

Her hand went up to her mouth and her eyes filled.

'When she had her heart surgery, I thought, 'This is it. This is when she will be taken from me.''

'Oh, Beth.'

'I still think it, still dread it the odd time, if I'm honest. That I'll lose her. You know, the world teaching me a lesson, an eye for an eye, or something?'

She hugged me hard. 'I let you down back then. Who knows what would have been, if I . . .'

'Don't, Mum.' I smiled at her and wiped a tear from my cheek. 'We live with it. And Mae's here now. And all she has done is love me without question from the very start. She gives and gives and gives. I should be more like her.'

A moment passed in silence before I spoke again.

'I think about your baby too, you know. My brother. And what that must have been like for you.'

'People didn't know what to say when a baby was stillborn.'

'So they said nothing?'

She nodded. 'A maternity hospital is the cruellest place on earth to be when you have no baby to celebrate.'

'Yes, I know.'

'There was the most dreadful silence around me for a few months. People didn't mention my baby and they didn't really ask after me either. Your father did his best with it but he wouldn't hear of having another child after that. So we didn't. That was his boy and he is loyal to his short life, such as it was.'

She brushed her hands down her skirt.

'Well, what doesn't kill you only makes you stronger. Isn't that what they say?'

I laughed. 'I've always thought that was a load of rubbish. What doesn't kill you will probably scar and weaken you. Or leave you nervous and fearful for the rest of your days.'

Now she was smiling. 'And teach you things you never wanted to learn.'

'Yes.'

'But it would be nice to believe it, wouldn't it?' She looked right at me.

'To believe that we don't live in a chaotic and unfair world? It would be great, Mum.' I squeezed her hand. 'Dad does love you. I'm sure of it.'

'Are you? That makes me feel better. You saying that.'

'Are you happy with how things are?

Generally speaking.'

'Well, I'm not unhappy. And that's a lot, I suppose. I'm happier for having this conversation.'

'It's always been difficult for us to be ourselves, I think, to speak freely with each other.'

'I will miss you, Beth. When you're gone.'

'I'll miss you too.' And I felt I really might.

'Best get back in. Your father will be looking for me.'

She went through the door ahead of me and the Ladies' President, Martha Somebody or Other, came toward us.

'There you are.' Martha stood next to me, very close, and took one of my hands. Quietly and slowly and with an odd intensity she said, 'You will always be very welcome in this club, Beth. Your whole family. Mae will always be welcome too.'

My daughter ran toward me, squeezed around my legs, and shouted 'I luvoo, Mama!' and ran away again, making aeroplane wings with her arms as she went. It was the perfect exchange; the fast and urgent need in her to hug me and the joy I got from it. My daughter knew more about living than I did. The particular emotion she felt in each moment was all she wanted to know.

She loved more and cared less. Perfect.

'That's lovely of you, Martha. Beth will be delighted to come back and visit us all here, won't you? And Mae too — how kind.'

I recognised that my mother hadn't the resources to live with Mae's difference without referring to it first. I recognised it because I had done it for so long myself.

I heard the doors slam again and, through the glass, I saw Gloria standing outside in her camel-coloured cashmere coat, her long hair loose on her shoulders, little fairy lights around her, hopping from foot to foot and tapping ash into her cupped palm.

⋆ ⋆ ⋆

It was getting late and Mae was sitting on Al's lap at the end of the room near the exit. Her hands were carefully splayed on an opened serviette on the table — two starfish — and Al was drawing around them with the pencil he always kept in his top pocket.

'Well, we'd better go to bed and let these people go home,' Steve said. It was the first witty thing I'd heard all evening.

I turned and waved a goodbye into the room.

Nobody noticed.

⋆ ⋆ ⋆

As we pulled out of our space in the car park, Steve was marvelling at the snow and suggesting plans for us tomorrow, if there was another fall overnight. I was distracted by an older couple leaning against a car at the far side of the darkened lot. Steve's animated voice faded almost to nothing as I stared at them and then everything around me, around them, dissolved. Something in the way their bodies fit together against the car. This man, leaning into this woman, her cashmere coat hanging by her sides. His arms out of view somewhere inside it. Their faces were hidden as our lights quickly passed over them but I knew the shape of the back of his head, his shoulders, his left leg — the side of his bad hip — stretched out, its polished shoe catching the light.

I had never seen him stand that close to his wife, my mother.

What I Will Remember

I finish the final stages of packing and shipping by bubble-wrapping a framed photo of us all — my mother and father, Steve, Al, Mae and me — the last thing to come down from our walls. It was professionally taken in a studio a year or so ago and shows the six of us from the torso up. A little cluster of happy, clear faces, necklines of bright pattern-less clothes against a white background. I think I've imagined it as something precious, a statement; a good family photo. But the frame holds just one particular second. Not the hours leading up to it, nor the minutes after.

From this photo, you'd never know that my mother had cried when my father announced an hour before that he wasn't going to the studio as 'we have enough photos', even though the time and date had already been changed twice to suit his schedule.

You'd never know that, in the end, he had come along reluctantly and opted to hold Mae in every shot. Or that for the short intervals between photos, he mostly just sat on the chair at the side with his hands linked together, staring down at the floor.

I am the head and chest between my parents, leaning to the right toward my father. My head is tilted that way and my right hand is to my ear because I lost an earring in the car on the way over. It might have been because I was turning it the way Steve said I did lately when I was tense.

Mae has her cheek pressed against my father's and is grinning. The very top of her scar peers out above the neck of her T-shirt; a sign of a struggle, of a triumph. Al is next to her, looking at her and laughing. Steve is next to him, facing forward wearing his best smile. My mother is on the far end, her everything-is-fabulous mask in place.

I walk through this house, less sure of itself now it's been stripped of its flesh. Only hints at the years of our life here remain. A chip out of the fireplace from a time when Al dropped a vase of flowers as he tried to set them down on the mantelpiece. I think of his crumpled face crying with embarrassment and worry and it makes me want to hug him, right now. The kitchen press above the toaster that is missing a handle since I slammed it after Steve first left us for those weeks — after I told him to. The two rubber black marks on the skirting board in the hall where Mae parked her doll's pram every evening for months before she went to bed.

Out our bedroom window upstairs, I see a grey sheet of darkness moving toward me, blackening the room and promising rain for the afternoon. I look across to the imposing gates of Vesey Hill; strong and proud, exerting their pressure. Here, where we are the unfortunate family with the little Down's girl.

I see Anna sitting at the window in her lounge, so well-turned-out and careful, her smile enhanced but with a desperation that leaks out from beneath it. She gave a little laugh yesterday when she said that I was 'finally giving in to Steve'.

'I suppose I am,' I said. Even though it doesn't feel that way.

'We always knew you wouldn't stay, that you didn't plan to,' she said, looking at Saoirse and Sommer.

'Why is that?'

'Because you never had any real work done on the house!' she said and sat back in her chair.

Saoirse nodded. Sommer looked aghast.

'You're here nearly ten years. All that time and you've not so much as knocked in the dividing walls!'

Moirah came back into the room. Her steel spindly heels clacking across the kitchen tiles.

'I was just saying to Beth how we knew

pretty quickly that she wasn't going to stay here. That she had other plans.'

'Oh yes. Sure, you never did anything to the house.'

Anna gave an idiotic little howl and for an awful moment I thought she might high-five Moirah.

'Maybe I just liked it as it was,' I said.

'We all like our houses as they are, Beth,' Saoirse said. 'But there are always things that can be done. It keeps you busy.'

'I can see how it could be exciting, in a way though. A big move,' Moirah said then. 'I mean, I couldn't dream of it. Ethan is four now and has really settled into his pre-school. And, as you know, since she got her place in Kings Primary, Chloe is doing really well. So we're firmly locked into 'The Education System'.' She did the inverted commas with her fingers thing. 'But I can see how it might appeal to some people who aren't as concerned about those things.'

'You've always been one part Vesey Hill, four parts . . . something else.' Anna spoke again.

'The services for Mae will be better in New Zealand,' Sommer said.

'She'll have more choices.' I nodded. 'And hopefully, I'll make some choices for myself too.'

'Oh, I'm going to miss you.' Sommer crossed the room and gave me a big and sudden hug. 'How will I manage here without you?' And her hugging me, and more so her doing it right then, in front of the linen trousers, made me love her more than ever.

The others left quickly enough after that.

'I wonder if I'll see this place differently, remember it in a different way, when I'm away from it?'

Sommer and I were sitting on my front step in our coats surveying the cul-de-sac before us.

'Unlikely,' she answered. 'I think you'll probably laugh.' She made a smoke ring with the wintry air.

'Thank you for your friendship,' I said.

'It has been my absolute pleasure.' She gave a little bow of her head.

Opposite, Robert came to his front door and stood looking out. His hair was oiled back with the clear lines of a comb impressively perfect and straight, the lump of him framed by the pair of great stone acorns on each side of his sliding porch. He nodded at us. We nodded back. A huge amount of nothing goes on in the suburbs.

'What did we *expect* when we moved here?' I asked Sommer quietly.

'I don't know. Maybe to be like those

women. You know, proper wives and mothers. With paint swatches and cupcake stands and outfits for the school gates.'

'Jesus.'

'I know.'

★ ★ ★

Later that evening, I come down the stairs running my hand along the wallpaper, taking in the thick dark carpet under my bare feet. And I think I sense someone brush against me, as though something I can't catch hold of, something I can't explain or don't know about, lingers in this house.

I sit down on the stairs and make myself consider some of the things that have happened over the last nine or ten years. And as I do, I feel how easily I can leave it all, how I can erase things in one go now like wipers on a window taking the rain away.

I remember Agnes in her hospital bed, speaking to me before I left, her voice tinny but clear. Telling me how I should be wherever I need to be and how she'd guide my path 'if that sort of thing is allowed, where I'm going. To be in the right place, with the right person, doing what feels right for you — I think that might be what it's all about. Start living, girl.'

It could have been terrifying to leave when the time came, like jumping off a careening bus. But it's now, and the bus has slowed to such a grinding pace that I see I'll be allowed an easy step and that I'll be relieved to take it. The need to leave runs simply and surely through me. Every day waiting to go now is a wasted day. I tilt my head up and give Agnes a little salute.

★   ★   ★

Mae is downstairs in the forever-unused dining room, wearing Steve's socks, running and sliding along the floors, empty now that the heavy furniture has been taken away. I have no memory of her ever venturing in here before. The heels of the socks are up around the back of her calves. She hears me come into the room and runs across the floor and jumps into my arms, laughing and squeezing me.

'Skating!' she says. 'Come on!' and I take off my shoes and we run and skid across the floor, filling this room with our laughter for the first time.

And I hope that this is what I will remember.

Kia hora te marino
Kia tere te karohirohi
Kia papapounamu te moana

Maori Blessing

May peace and calmness surround you,
May you reside in the warmth of
a summer's haze,
May the ocean of your travels be as
smooth as the polished greenstone.

Translation

2015

So we crossed our fingers and stepped off the bus.

It's late March now and the days are warm still. I stand on the porch of the white wooden house where we live and look out at the wild, red bursts from the tree at the front of it. From here, with my blue cup in my hand, I can see central Auckland, the tips of the coloured triangular sails stretching up into the sky, the busyness of the harbour — life happening right there at the end of the street. This house feels like me, like us. We talk in this house, Steve and I, Al and Mae. We make plans together, plans for our future. I feel clear now — a ball shot from a cannon.

My mother and I speak occasionally on the phone and I think she sounds as far away as she is. Steve and I are free or we have been let go, I'm not sure which. She and my father have mentioned coming out to see the children and maybe one day they will. I emailed them a photo of our house and my mother has it as the background on her mobile phone. She told me that Julie Brooks was back from America for a holiday when I sent it, so it was good timing. She didn't tell her we were 'only renting' it.

As I think about my parents, I hear the sound of our wheels crushing the carpet of stones on their driveway as we drove out their gate for the last time. I think of how barely I miss that place, even in the most routine kind of way. I think of my mother trying to play basketball with Al around the back of her house before we left for the airport, an attempt to involve herself in what he wanted to do for the first time. So clumsy and eager and late with her efforts.

And how she spoke to me — 'People think me quite an upbeat and optimistic person, Beth. But that positivity isn't always what I'm feeling, I think you know that. In fact, I think it might often be fear. Well, sometimes.' She turned her earring and looked away. 'Fear that one day something will be pointed out to me, something that I won't be able to clean up once it's been spoken aloud. Like you said to me that afternoon you got cross about the magnet in the kitchen — that I'm always trying to tidy life away. You were right.'

She would have been easy to deceive, I suppose, because love ignores what doesn't suit it. And in loving my father so much, she had given him the confidence to think highly of himself, the confidence to be entitled to someone else.

I think about my father tapping at his watch face with his nail when I mentioned cutting a slice of cake, that last day in their kitchen, in the house that I grew up in. My back was turned to him but I saw his reflection in the oven door. And I remember how she pushed her chair back that instant and took a final drink from her cup as quickly as its heat would allow.

'Well, we'd better all get going then,' she'd said.

And I remember the words she spoke into my hair as she clasped me at the airport: 'I envy you. I could never take a risk like this. I don't have anything I can believe in enough to take a risk for it.'

'Ready?' Steve had asked me. He was carrying Mae on his back.

'I think so.'

His smile, so broad, made me smile.

He took my hand. 'Let's do this.'

As Al linked me on the other side and we moved to turn away, my father put a supportive arm around my mother's shoulders and held it there.

She is the habit of his lifetime.

★ ★ ★

301

I rang home earlier this morning and my mother answered the phone laughing. It was Saturday evening in Ireland and Annabel from the club was with her.

'We've had a lovely afternoon, Annabel and I. The weather is fine here, for this time of year. We went for a walk into the village and I met that nice lady, your neighbour Moirah. She was asking for you.'

'Oh, yes?'

'She said she hoped you had managed to find a school that would be prepared to take Mae.'

Before I had a chance to answer, I heard my father's voice behind her. 'I think somebody in here offered me a cup of coffee — sure it must be ten minutes ago now?'

I told my mother I had to go because the paper boy was at the door.

'Oooooh. A paper boy? How very American. And on a Sunday morning? That's a great service. I must tell Julie. Anyway, I'd better go too — your father needs me.'

I was smiling as I said goodbye.

Already it feels like new, freckled skin has grown over an old wound. I live my life differently now, with this distance, knowing my parents aren't watching. Knowing I can't watch them.

Later this year, Sommer and Rashid, Issa and Ibrahim will be here for a holiday. Sommer laughed telling me that they could afford to come because they were the only ones who hadn't bought their house, the only ones in Vesey Hill without negative equity.

The blue cup I'm holding is one of the few things I didn't put into storage when we left there. It is still only ever in my hand or upturned on the draining board. All the other things, the big things I needed around me then, things I thought I couldn't bear to part with, that I needed in order to cope, remain stored. Neither needed nor even missed. I look around our wooden house for some other influence of that life before, for some sign of all my years on the opposite side of the world, but I can't see it. With nothing to hold it, the memory of our time in Vesey Hill has slid away.

★ ★ ★

Small things I will always remember: Anna's voice loud and clear and always sure of itself, her pinched little face and the accordion of tiny lines around her mouth. The way Steve rubbed his hand back and forward across his forehead on our last day when she came over to say goodbye. I'll remember the way her tone changed and her words quickened when he went around the side to lock up the gates and she quietly suggested that I try to manage without an au pair because 'You know Steve.' The way she dabbed her fingernail on her bottom lip and added, 'I'd worry he might, well, *take to her* a little too much.' Then that smile.

The feeling of something cold sliding over me and filling my stomach when she reminded me how Robert 'travels a lot for work too' and how he had seen Steve in the airport hotel in London one night, some time ago now, 'with a good-looking blonde woman'. And how 'it took Steve rather a while to notice him though' because he was 'so *preoccupied* with her'. Again that smile.

'Honestly, Beth, after Robert told me, I agonised about it. I barely slept! I had to confide in Saoirse and Moirah, and you can't imagine how much we debated the whole thing. In the end, Moirah and I agreed that we should tell you, that you should know about her before you left. In case you didn't already? Saoirse didn't see the point of us getting involved but, well, we didn't want you making a mistake, cutting yourself off from your friends! Leaving everything you have here for him.' Smile.

I will remember her standing on my cobblelocked doorstep, with only minutes left to go, pulling the pin from the grenade, trying to explode my new life. And how I answered her before I shut the door: 'I already know about her. Her name is Jane. But thank you and fuck you, Anna.'

★ ★ ★

So here we are, the four of us — the Rogers of Parnell, Auckland. And at forty-five, I feel freedom for the first time. I see now that I wasn't that different at all from the linen trousers brigade; I had become just as small and resentful and bored as they were. Losing myself in empty routines. I like myself better now, where the cinder bowl of Mount Eden is at my back. The quiet damp is leaving our bones here, where the air is warm.

I'm reading a lot. Like I did years ago, back before life folded over on itself. I've even started writing stories of my own again. With an enthusiasm and a purpose that feels brand new. Early in the mornings and late in the evenings out here on the porch. And in May, I start a new job as a copywriter.

Al comes from the kitchen in his shorts and collapses his giant body onto the swing chair.

He is nearly seventeen and is settling into himself.

'I know it's not a big thing, Mum, but do you know what's great?' His voice is deep and, with a slight accent to it now, he sounds more like his father. 'I love that I don't have to wear a jacket the whole year round.'

Steve comes out too, overhearing.

'You all like it here. I knew it!' He puts his arms around my waist and rests his chin on my shoulder.

'Don't even try to tell me that you don't,' he says softly into my ear.

I smile and sip my tea.

He and I have secrets from each other, but they don't belong here. I think of Jane and Eoin and bad choices. I think back to 1986 and the secret kept by my mother and me and a middle-aged man I haven't spoken to in nearly twenty-nine years. I let it all go. Across the water with the coloured sails.

We hear Mae getting out of bed, her feet thump-thumping onto the floor.

I think how I used to have two anxieties around her, both running side by side like rivers flowing into and out of each other, babbling for prominence: the immediate river — how to get through this next hour with her, this trip to the supermarket, this walk down the street; and then the deeper and darker waters — what would become of her when I died? Where would she be in fifty years' time and what would it mean for Al?

Those rivers have run themselves dry.

She appears on the deck barefoot in her pyjamas, her eyes scrunched against the early sun, looking at me. She holds all of herself, all of her love, in her outstretched arms. She runs to me and we all feel it.

Acknowledgements

Thank you to:

- Ciara Doorley for her positivity and un-wavering belief;
- Vanessa Fox-O'Loughlin for making fortu-itous introductions;
- The Tyrone Guthrie Centre and everyone at Annaghmakerrig, where much of this book was written;
- Yvonne Cullen for being demanding, in the very best way, and Ruth Hickey for being an intelligent reader and a straight talker.
- Huge gratitude to my parents for not being like Beth's, and to Matthew and my children for being everything.

We do hope that you have enjoyed reading this large print book.

Did you know that all of our titles are available for purchase?

We publish a wide range of high quality large print books including:
Romances, Mysteries, Classics
General Fiction
Non Fiction and Westerns

Special interest titles available in large print are:
The Little Oxford Dictionary
Music Book
Song Book
Hymn Book
Service Book

Also available from us courtesy of Oxford University Press:
Young Readers' Dictionary
(large print edition)
Young Readers' Thesaurus
(large print edition)

For further information or a free brochure, please contact us at:
Ulverscroft Large Print Books Ltd.,
The Green, Bradgate Road, Anstey,
Leicester, LE7 7FU, England.
Tel: (00 44) 0116 236 4325
Fax: (00 44) 0116 234 0205

Other titles published by Ulverscroft:

GREY SOULS

Philippe Claudel

France, December 1917: Daily life continues in a small town near the Front, despite the pounding of artillery fire and the parade of wounded strangers passing through its streets. Then any lingering sense of normality is destroyed with the discovery of a strangled ten-year-old girl in the freezing canal. A deserter is convicted of her murder and executed, and the case closed. Years later, one man is still trying to make sense of these events, while struggling with the tragedies and demons of his own past. But excavating the town's secret history will bring neither peace nor justice . . .